The Literary Adventures of Sherlock Holmes:

A Collection of Short Sketches

Volume Two

[Containing additional manuscripts found in the dispatch box of
Dr John H. Watson
In the vault of Cox & Co., Charing Cross, London]

Edited

By

Daniel D. Victor, Ph.D.

Paperback ISBN 978-1-78705-466-0
ePub ISBN 978-1-78705-467-7
PDF ISBN 978-1-78705-468-4

MX Publishing
335 Princess Park Manor, Royal Drive,
London, N11 3GX
www.mxpublishing.com

Cover design by Brian Belanger

Also by Daniel D. Victor

The Seventh Bullet:
The Further Adventures of Sherlock Holmes

A Study in Synchronicity

The Final Page of Baker Street
(Book One in the series,
Sherlock Holmes and the American Literati)

Sherlock Holmes and the Baron of Brede Place
(Book Two in the series,
Sherlock Holmes and the American Literati)

Seventeen Minutes to Baker Street
(Book Three in the series,
Sherlock Holmes and the American Literati)

The Outrage at the Diogenes Club
(Book Four in the series,
Sherlock Holmes and the American Literati)

Sherlock Holmes and the Shadows of St Petersburg

Sherlock Holmes and the London Particular
(Book Five in the series,
Sherlock Holmes and the American Literati)

For David Marcum,
without whose encouragement
these stories would never have seen the light of day

Introduction

As compiled by Arthur Conan Doyle, the original cases of Sherlock Holmes may be categorized in any number of ways. There are, for example, those that feature animals such as *The Hound of the Baskervilles*, "The Veiled Lodger," and "The Lion's Mane." Others, like "A Case of Identity" and "The Noble Bachelor," may be labeled as stories of love gone awry. Some, like "The Three Garridebs" and "The Dancing Men," feature American villains. And still others, like "The Second Stain" and "The Bruce Partington Plans," depict political subterfuge.

The eleven stories gathered together in this two-volume anthology share their own common feature. All have connections to the world of *belles lettres*, the world of literature—some to authors in particular, others to themes or stories associated with specific writers.

In both volumes, the stories appear in the chronological order of the cases they depict. Those in Volume One take place before Sherlock Holmes reappears from his presumed death at the Reichenbach Falls. The stories in the second volume proceed well into his retirement.

By way of introduction to the stories, allow me to establish their literary associations:

- "The Missing Necklace" tells of Holmes's friendship with French author, Guy de Maupassant, which led to the writing of one of the French author's most famous stories.

- "The Amateur Emigrant" pairs Holmes with Robert Louis Stevenson on the single night the writer spent in New York City.

- "The Second William Wilson" serves as a sequel to a frightening psychological tale by Edgar Allan Poe.

- "The Aspen Papers" offers Watson's account of a situation that Henry James fictionalized in his acclaimed short story, "The Aspern Papers."

- "For Want of a Sword" and "Capitol Murder" identify the role of Sherlock Holmes in two historical events—one involving the British Navy in the Mediterranean; the other, the assassination of an American governor—both occurrences originally reported by American journalist and novelist, David Graham Phillips.

- "The Smith-Mortimer Succession" that begins Volume Two illustrates a case referenced by Holmes's Boswell-like biographer, Dr John Watson, in "The Golden Pince-Nez."

- "An Adventure in Darkness" completes the story about the country of the blind first made public by author H.G. Wells.

- "An Adventure in the Mid-Day Sun" presents a case in the voice of the young American mystery writer Raymond Chandler, who in his youth served as a page-boy at 221B Baker Street.

- "The Star-Crossed Lovers," like the title, echoes the primary theme of Shakespeare's *Romeo and Juliet*.

- Finally, "A Case of Mistaken Identity" documents the meeting between Sherlock Holmes and the American novelist F. Scott Fitzgerald that took place late in the detective's life.

Let others plumb this collection for more subtle themes. From Maupassant to Fitzgerald, the authorial giants who populate the pages of both volumes are explanation enough for its title. As interesting as such literary associations may be, of course, one can never forget that these sketches depict a series of heartless criminal acts—some more gruesome than others—in the finest tradition of all the other adventures of Sherlock Holmes.

Daniel D. Victor, Ph.D.
Los Angeles, California
June 2019

Sources

"The Adventure of the Missing Necklace" originally appeared in *The MX Book of New Sherlock Holmes Stories, Part IV,* ed. David Marcum, (London: MX Publishing, 2016).

"The Adventure of the Amateur Emigrant" originally appeared in *Sherlock Holmes: Before Baker Street,* ed. Derrick Belanger (Manchester, NH: Belanger Books LLC, 2017).

"The Adventure of the Second William Wilson" originally appeared in *The MX Book of New Sherlock Holmes Stories, Part VII,* ed. David Marcum (London: MX Publishing, 2017).

"The Adventure of the Aspen Papers" originally appeared in *The MX Book of New Sherlock Holmes Stories, Part I,* ed. David Marcum (London: MX Publishing, 2015).

"For Want of a Sword" originally appeared in Holmes *Away from Home: Adventures from the Great Hiatus, Volume Two,* ed. David Marcum (Manchester, NH: Belanger Books, LLC , 2016).

"The Adventure of the Smith-Mortimer Succession" originally appeared in *The MX Book of New Sherlock Holmes Stories, Part XII* ed. David Marcum (London: MX Publishing, 2018).

"Capitol Murder" originally appeared in *The MX Book of New Sherlock Holmes Stories, Part X,* ed. David Marcum (London: MX Publishing, 2018).

"An Adventure in Darkness" originally appeared in *Sherlock Holmes: Adventures in the Realms of H.G. Wells, Volume 1,* ed. Derrick Belanger and C. Edward Davis (Manchester, NH: Belanger Books, LLC , 2017).

"An Adventure in the Mid-Day Sun" originally appeared in *Beyond Watson: A Sherlock Holmes Anthology of Stories NOT Told by Dr John H. Watson,* ed. Derrick Belanger (Manchester, NH: Belanger Books LLC, 2016).

"The Adventure of the Star-Crossed Lovers" originally appeared in *Sherlock Holmes: Adventures Beyond the Canon, Vol. 3*, ed. Derrick Belanger (Manchester, NH: Belanger Books LLC, 2018).

"A Case of Mistaken Identity" originally appeared in *The MX Book of New Sherlock Holmes Stories, Part VI,* ed. David Marcum (London: MX Publishing, 2017).

A Note on the Text

Footnotes followed by (JHW) were supplied by Dr. John H. Watson. Footnotes followed by (DDV) were supplied by the editor.

Table of Contents

Volume One

Volume Two

The Adventure of the Smith-Mortimer Succession

The famous Smith-Mortimer succession case
comes also within this period [1894].
--Dr John H. Watson
"The Adventure of the
Golden Pince-Nez"

*N*o detective, not even an amateur, wants to admit that he has been the victim of thieves. And yet that was precisely the situation in which I found myself after moving back to Baker Street in May of 1894, some two weeks after the dramatic return from the dead of my friend and colleague, Mr Sherlock Holmes.

By now the whole world knows the astounding story of how Holmes had appeared to plunge to his death at the Reichenbach Falls in Switzerland on 4 May 1891, how he had spent the next three years travelling incognito, and how he had finally reappeared in London in the spring of '94 to solve the murder of one Ronald Adair. Though today such facts are readily available, it must be remembered that for reasons never made entirely clear to me, Holmes prohibited my publishing an account of the case for some ten years following his resurrection.

Adhering to Holmes's request, I waited patiently until the autumn of '03—actually, a year prior to the end of his self-proclaimed moratorium—when he finally allowed me to produce the sketch I entitled "The Empty House", the narrative that detailed Holmes's so-called "hiatus".

Though he had made it quite clear that my account was not to be published for a decade, I stood firm about recording the facts as soon as Holmes reported them to me—that is, in April of '94. Only by noting the details while they were still fresh in my mind, I told him, would I be able to fulfil the role of faithful Boswell that he had attributed to me.

To that end, I maintained a notebook in which I set down the salient features of the Reichenbach affair as soon as Holmes provided them to me. I kept the thin volume in a drawer of the writing desk in our sitting room, and it was the purloining of the notebook in question that placed me in the predicament to which I referred at the start of this narrative.

I discovered the theft one balmy afternoon in late May. It happened this way. Upon returning from my surgery, I encountered the perfect opportunity to write. There was no Sherlock Holmes to be found, and an hour yet remained before Mrs Hudson would bring up our tea. No sooner had I seated myself, however, than I opened the desk-drawer and discovered that my notebook had gone missing.

I immediately summoned Billy the page. "Has anyone entered our rooms recently when Mr Holmes and I have been out?" I asked him.

"Why, um, yeh, Doctor," said the boy, tugging self-consciously at his burgundy tunic. "Funny you should ask."

"And why is that?"

Billy shifted uneasily from foot to foot. "Some bloke, a young fellow 'e was and very short, come in yesterday with a bucket and sponge—said 'e was 'ere to wash the windows."

"And you," I charged in disbelief, "let him in without so much as a 'by your leave'?"

Billy blushed, unable to conceal his miscalculation. "Mrs H was out, Doctor, so I couldn't ask no one about the fella's story. Both you and Mr 'olmes was gone; and, strange enough, the chap sounded like an educated fellow. I reckoned no 'arm could be done, so I opened your door for 'im. You know 'ow Mrs H allows the police inspectors free run of the place."

"Window cleaners are not Scotland Yard detectives, Billy," said I, shaking my head in annoyance. "You should be aware, young man, that this window cleaner took an important notebook that belonged to me."

Rather than apologizing for his blunder, Billy raised a forefinger and said, "Do you know, Doctor, I thought something seemed a bit dodgy about 'im—besides 'is posh speech."

"And why is that?" I said, my voice tinged with irritation.

"Because 'e 'aint been in 'ere but five minutes, and then out 'e rushed, bucket in 'and, saying 'ow 'e forgot 'is soap, and just like that 'e runs out the front door."

Now that Billy mentioned it, the begrimed windows looked no different from the day before. The strange behaviour of the window cleaner certainly seemed to confirm the intruder's guilt.

Whilst I could not let Billy leave without admonishing him for his poor judgement, I also found myself thanking him for offering so straightforward an admission. Only after the lad had gone did I stop to consider the peculiarity of the theft. Nothing else seemed missing, and I had no clue concerning what vital interest there could be in my simple notes of Holmes's return to London. They contained no secrets.

If the details of Holmes's escape from Moriarty's clutches were not already public knowledge, Holmes's reappearance in the fight against London's criminal class most certainly was. How could it not be? Elsewhere I have noted the many cases he tackled in 1894, and his presence was obviously known to all the participants in each of those investigations. One need not be a Yarder to understand that word travels quickly among the denizens of London's underworld when it comes to matters of survival.

Holmes himself returned in time for tea, and I related to him the mystery involving my notes.

"Curious, Watson," said he, cocking an eyebrow. "But 'tis no great matter. Disturbing as it is to be the victim of a minor crime, no major harm can come from missing the notes of my reappearance. I shall merely repeat the details for you, and you may take them down again. Fear not. I have no doubt that with the passage of time your little puzzle will be solved."

Although we did not know it that afternoon as we sat sampling Mrs Hudson's tea and biscuits, the solution to that so-called "little puzzle" was destined to appear much sooner and with greater implications than we ever could have imagined.

*****

It was a week to the day since I had discovered the thievery in our sitting room, and I had almost succeeded in pushing the matter out of mind. Having questioned Holmes about his escape from Moriarty once more and recorded for a second time the facts required to complete a satisfactory account of his actions in Switzerland, I no longer had the need to dwell upon what I had come to call "The Singular Case of the Missing Notebook". That morning, in fact, along with the breakfast dishes and the coffee, Billy presented a letter that had been left for Holmes. Such communications usually suggested new cases, and thus I felt doubly certain that more weighty issues would replace my concern over a loss that no longer mattered.

"Brought in early this morning by a footman in livery, sir," said Billy on his way out the door.

My friend examined the envelope with its thick-stock paper, overly large monogram, and red-wax seal.

"Someone important," said he with a wry chuckle, "or at least someone who thinks he is." Holmes broke the seal and quickly scanned the letter. "Note the shaky hand in contrast to the firmest of tones," he said as he pushed the paper in my direction. It was dated that morning at Windstone Hall, Gloucestershire.

Dear Mr Holmes [it read],

I shall meet with you this morning at 11.00 in your rooms. It is of the utmost urgency, and I must insist that you cancel any other plans you might have.

It was signed, *"Sir Lionel Smith-Mortimer, Bart".*

"Watson," Holmes said over the rim of his coffee cup, "The *Who's Who?* if you please."

I gulped down a piece of toast and rose to fetch A.C. Black's familiar listing of influential people. It took but a moment to locate the book with its dark-blue boards and gold-lettered spine. I thumbed the pages, found the appropriate entry, and handed the open volume to Holmes.

Sipping his coffee, he read the passage quickly and summarised the salient features for me: "Lionel Smith-Mortimer, Baronet. Born 1822. One son named Leigh. Wife died in childbirth. In addition to an inherited title and fortune, he is the owner of Windstone Hall, a manor house in Oxfordshire. He—"

"Wait a moment, Holmes!" I cried. "I remember reading something about the son called Leigh just yesterday in the *Times*—a rather tragic piece about a suicide, as I recall." I retrieved the newspaper from the small pile of spent dailies residing on a nearby table. It took me but a moment to locate the report. "Here!" said I, pointing to the story. It was indeed a melancholy announcement—"Death of Baronet's Son"—so sad an account that I had not gone on to read the details. Had I done so, I would certainly have called them to my friend's attention.

"Holmes," said I after quickly reviewing the piece, "it says that the young man died in the Falls of Reichenbach."

Sherlock Holmes put down his cup and stared at me with his steel-grey eyes.

"'The coat of the deceased,'" I read aloud, "'was discovered neatly folded on the path above the falls. His footprints along the path led to the edge of the precipice above the water—a drop of more than eight hundred feet. His body has yet to be recovered.'"

I laid down the paper and looked at my friend. If I did not know better, I could have sworn that the slightly upturned corners of Holmes's mouth displayed a hint of amusement.

"I returned from death but a month ago," said Holmes, "and already I seem to have created imitators." He looked at our mantel clock. "Come. It is almost eleven; and unless my ears are very much mistaken, a pair of disciplined horses are pulling a four-wheeler to the kerb. We should prepare to meet our distinguished guest."

Sherlock Holmes exchanged his mouse-coloured dressing gown for a dark jacket, and I proceeded to don my coat. It was a matter of minutes before Mrs Hudson herself climbed the stairs to introduce our guest. No page-boys for the likes of a Baronet.

"Enter!" Sherlock Holmes commanded at her knock.

Mrs Hudson opened the door and stood at the portal. "Sir Lionel Smith-Mortimer," she announced. Then bowing her head, she straightened her skirt, backed out into the hallway, and closed the door.

I must say that whilst I knew this Baronet to be a septuagenarian, I nonetheless expected to behold someone of erect and noble bearing. Instead, I saw before us a scowling old man with a stoop to his back and a hand curled like a great claw over the round, silver head of his walking stick. With a nod to fashion, he wore an expertly tailored suit, its dark frock coat contrasting with his yellowing white hair. Patent leather boots complemented his attire.

"Sir Lionel," said my friend, "I am Sherlock Holmes." He introduced me as well and gestured towards the armchair Holmes reserved for his clients.

The Baronet gave a quick frown in my direction and then with some effort shuffled to the proffered seat, and sat down. Holmes and I took chairs opposite him.

"Let me first say, sir," announced the elderly client with a thump of his stick, "that I don't fancy being here one bit." He rapped his stick on the floor a second time to punctuate his point. "Only because of Leigh's faith in you have I come at all."

Holmes stared at the man, offering no discernible response.

"Without doubt you have seen the reports of my son's accident."

We both nodded respectfully.

"Simply put, I don't believe them. I want to know what really happened. All I do know is that he was wandering about in Switzerland with a friend."

"A friend?" Holmes asked.

"Yes. One Reginald Bentley. A barrister by profession. Known each other for about a year. Bentley and my son travel together when the opportunity presents itself. London not good enough for them. They want to see the world."

"And where was this Bentley at the time of your son's death?" Holmes asked.

"*Alleged* death, may I remind you. He remained at the hotel near the Reichenbach Falls, don't you know."

"At the *Englischer Hof*?" I asked. Noting the similarity to our own ill-fated trip three years before, I guessed the two men might have stayed in the same hotel Holmes and I had occupied.

As if he believed I possessed too much arcane information, Sir Lionel knit his brow. But all he said was, "By Jove, when I hear of a mysterious death and no corpse is produced, I have my doubts. You may think I sound like some suspicious figure in one of your adventures, Holmes, but that may be in part because of the interest that Leigh expressed in reading about them."

"I appreciate the kind words, Sir Lionel," said Holmes, ignoring the fact that the compliment might better have been directed at the author of those adventures. "But under the circumstances," Holmes went on, "one cannot escape an uncomfortable conclusion. The apparent death of your son mirrors—however imprecisely—my own rumoured demise. Given the fact that I myself have only just returned from that narrow escape, one has to marvel at the coincidence."

"Quite," muttered Sir Lionel.

It was at that moment that the thought of my missing notes popped back into my head. The young man posing as a window cleaner whom Billy had observed, the one with an educated manner of speech—might he be none other than Leigh Smith-Mortimer whose father now sat before us? Recreating the death of Sherlock Holmes, someone he admired, could have been his morbid motivation. Perhaps Leigh Smith-Mortimer had sought to end his brief life in dramatic fashion not unlike the storied suicide of the Romantic poet Thomas Chatterton who succumbed to arsenic at the age of seventeen.

"I must confess," said Holmes, "that the role of my personal history in this situation adds impetus to my curiosity. I too would like to know what happened to your son, Sir Lionel. I shall take your case."

The Baronet withdrew a wallet of light-coloured leather from inside his jacket. "Name your fee, Holmes," said he.

"Later," my friend replied. "All my clients pay at the same rate, Sir Lionel. But concerning this case in particular, its proper resolution will furnish me with additional reward."

The Baronet gazed at his wallet. "I almost forgot," said he, extracting a photograph and a small card from the billfold. "My son and Bentley," he explained in reference to the photograph, "inseparable friends. The card contains information about Bentley's chambers in Gray's Inn."

Holmes took the items, examined them briefly, and handed them to me. In the photograph, two serious-looking young men in straw boaters—the taller one with a moustache, the shorter, clean-shaven—stared back."

"Leigh is the one without the whiskers," said Sir Lionel as, using his stick as a brace, he struggled to rise. "As for Bentley, he works at Mapplethorpe and Ruggles, and I have already prepared him for your visit at 2.00 this afternoon. He awaits you in Gray's Inn Gardens."

"That gives us a half hour," said Holmes in spite of the old man's presumptuousness. "We must leave poste haste," he added, ushering Sir Lionel to the door.

But the Baronet had more to say and stopped to address my friend. "This matter is of great importance to me, Holmes. In addition to the welfare of my son, I feel compelled to point out that he is my only issue. He arrived late in my life, and his mother died tragically during his birth. It was quite horrible really. The babe chose to appear when Lady Smith-Mortimer and I were vacationing in the mountains near Lake Windermere. It was all so sudden. We were alone in the woods, and I had to deliver the child myself as my wife lay dying."

"Horrible," I said.

Sir Lionel ignored my response. "What's more," he added, standing up as straight as seemed possible for him, "neither can I neglect the deposition of my estate."

"It is entailed?" Holmes asked.

"Indeed. All I possess will be inherited by my closest male heir. If Leigh is truly no longer living, then Windstone Hall will be dealt off to some distant cousin in Canada. That is why it is imperative that I find out what happened to my son."

"Understood," said Holmes. "I will report to you as soon as I learn anything."

We listened as Sir Lionel made his way down the seventeen steps, his walking stick producing a distinctive thump on each one.

I heard the latch of the carriage door and then the clatter of the wheels as Sir Lionel's four-wheeler drove off down Baker Street.

"Come, Watson," said Holmes, already moving towards the door. "We shall begin this investigation with our pre-arranged interview of Mr Reginald Bentley, Esquire, the travelling companion of Leigh Smith-Mortimer."

*****

We flagged a hansom at our front door and were soon rattling along Oxford Street. Southampton Row brought us to High Holborn and the Inns of Court, the legal centre of London. We alighted at the wood-panelled frontage of the Cittie of Yorke public house that stands at the narrow alleyway leading to Gray's Inn. Entering the grounds through the main gate, we passed the South Square to our right and made our way under the archway leading to the green swards of the Walks, as the spacious Gray's Inn Gardens are more commonly called.

It had just gone 2.00, and under the afternoon sun we walked quickly along the gravel path enveloped by the iridescent colours and sweet aromas of the season. Spring seems so wrong a time to hold discussions of death— especially among the yellow daffodils and blue hyacinths and roses of pink and white and red attempting to distract us. After a few additional paces, however, we recognised the moustachioed chap from the photograph seated on a nearby bench.

Reginald Bentley was sitting in the shade of the London-planes and elms that populated the Walks, and he rose upon our arrival. "Gentlemen," said he, "Thank you for agreeing to see me outside of chambers. This tragedy is no one's business but our own." He pointed to a low-slung block of yellow-brick offices across the lawn. "Besides, Mapplethorpe and Ruggles have suffered the confinement of the Raymond Buildings over there since the early years of the century. I appreciate the moments I can spend away from my desk. As you must already know, Leigh and I always enjoyed our walks through the countryside."

"Which leads us to the Falls of Reichenbach," said Holmes. "As I understand it, your friend seemed intrigued by my personal history—so much so that he literally walked in my very footsteps. How does one account for this obsessive interest?"

"Let us sit," said Bentley, gesturing towards the bench. "Justice was paramount for Leigh," he explained once we were settled. "I should imagine his concern was based upon his own sense of victimhood."

"Victimhood?" I echoed, imagining the rich surroundings of Windstone Hall in which the boy had grown up. "In what way?"

"I know what you're thinking, Dr Watson—the money that must have smothered Leigh when he was a child. But, you see, it was that very legacy that constantly weighed him down. His father had made it clear to Leigh that he had to marry and have sons to carry on the line—you know, gentlemen, the usual upper-class prattle."

"You don't approve of the British aristocracy?" I could not refrain from asking.

"Look," he said, "my own father is a banker and fortunately for me was able to send me to university. I have benefitted greatly from my education. After all, here I sit, installed in the legal profession and quite able to pay my own bills."

"Rather proves my point, eh?" I said.

"Within reason, Doctor. I don't believe one should be forced to live the life one's father confers upon him however much money that involves if that is not the life one chooses for himself."

The young man may have had a valid point for the common fellow, but one cannot allow the upper classes to make such choices. Where would we be if the heirs to the throne could choose willy-nilly whether they wanted to be king? One could scarcely imagine a royal monarch giving up the crown to marry a commoner! Of course, such dilemmas did not concern a mere medical man like myself—not that sort of money in my family, I am afraid.

Holmes brought the conversation back to practicalities. "Tell me about this trip the two of you took to Switzerland."

Bentley patted down his moustache. "When Sir Lionel notified me that you'd be coming to talk about Leigh, I assumed you would ask about that final journey." He withdrew a map from an inner pocket and, unfolding it, proceeded to lay the sheet flat on the bench between Holmes and himself. "Leigh invited me to join him with the understanding that I would follow his instructions without questioning them. He told me he had a plan, and I agreed to go along."

Sherlock Holmes studied the chart, his eyes flashing as he noted the familiar route now coloured in red.

"I took the liberty to mark our course," said Bentley. "It was a singular excursion." As the young man spoke, he traced the progress of their trip with his forefinger. "We boarded the *Continental Express* here at Victoria. I had originally thought we would cross the Channel at Dover and sail the twenty-two miles to Calais, but Leigh had other plans. He insisted we change trains at Canterbury for the run to Newhaven, a decision that caused us to switch twice more at Ashford and Lewes. When I asked him why, he answered with your name, Mr Holmes."

"Quite so," Holmes nodded. "Pray, continue."

"I'm sure you yourself can supply the details. At Newhaven, we sailed to Dieppe,"—here Bentley's finger on the map slid across the blue of the Channel—"a crossing, I might add, three times the duration of the crossing at Dover. From Dieppe we travelled by train to Brussels and then on to Strasbourg and Geneva. Following a week's walk through the Rhone Valley, we made our way to Leuk, climbed the Gemmi Pass in the Central Alps, and finally arrived just a short distance from the Reichenbach Falls in a town called Meiringen. We stayed in the *Englischer Hof* run by—"

"Let me guess," I interrupted, "Peter Steiler the elder."

"Correct, Dr Watson. But from what I understand, you and Mr Holmes stayed in the same hotel."

"Quite so," said Holmes again. Then he added vaguely, "It was all done for professional reasons."

Leigh Smith-Mortimer may have stolen my notes concerning the geographical route Holmes and I had taken to Meiringen, but obviously Holmes still wanted to conceal the details connected with the criminal activities of Professor Moriarty and his associate Colonel Moran.

"To be sure, gentlemen, we had travelled a great distance in a roundabout fashion; and yet we finally did reach our destination, and so I could fathom no reason to suddenly start doubting my friend's sanity. Thus, when early the next morning Leigh told me he wished to go alone to view the Reichenbach Falls, I acquiesced. It was the last time I would ever see him." Here Reginald Bentley hung his head. Had I been less sympathetic, I might have regarded it as an altogether too theatrical a pose.

"And then?" Holmes asked. "No doubt you alerted the police."

"When Leigh failed to return, I myself walked up to the Falls—ran, really."

I nodded with appreciation. Had I not made the same fateful run under the most similar of conditions?

"That," Bentley resumed, "was when I found Leigh's folded jacket and tweed cap lying at the end of the small path leading to the rushing waters. Once I saw those personal items, I suspected that something was truly wrong, and I summoned the police. We all returned to the scene, and they examined the footmarks leading to the edge and not returning. Alas, there was but one sad conclusion to draw—that Leigh had thrown himself from the precipice, his body disappearing in the churning waters below."

Holmes arched his eyebrows. "It would certainly seem so," said he. "Did you detect anything in Leigh's nature that would lead you to imagine he could perform such an act?"

Sighing heavily, Bentley stared up into the cloudless blue sky. Perhaps he was hoping to find an answer somewhere in the heavens. "I can only tell you that he hated the role his father had placed him in. But I assure you, gentlemen, that I never suspected that Leigh was unhappy enough to do himself in. There's really not much else I have to say on the subject—except that I miss my friend greatly."

Holmes stood up. "Thank you, Mr Bentley. You've been a great help to us."

The barrister collected his map and gently folded it along the creases. Replacing it in his coat pocket, he shook hands with the two of us and wished us well. We accompanied him as far as his chambers and then bade him good day.

"Do you realise, Watson," said Holmes once we reached High Holborn, "that thanks to Mr Bentley—not to mention the dead Mr Smith-Mortimer—we are going to have to return to the scene of some of our most unpleasant memories?" When he raised his hand to flag a hansom, he bore the gravest of expressions.

*****

Unlike our first trip to the Reichenbach Falls, we required no subterfuge on this occasion. We faced no adversary like Moriarty in his special train to fool into thinking we were going to Paris. The *Express* from Victoria took us directly to Dover. From there, a ship conveyed us to Calais. With no need to pose as carefree pedestrians touring the Valley of the Rhone or exploring the Alps of central Switzerland, we utilised the various railroads traversing the French and Swiss countrysides to deposit us at the chalet-like train station in Meiringen.

Holmes and I may not have looked like the tourists we had hoped to resemble three years before, but even on that earlier occasion we had no cause to conceal our true identities. When we reached the *Englischer Hof*, therefore, old Peter Steiler greeted Holmes in particular like an old friend.

"*Ach*, Herr Holmes," said Steiler, his English helped by an earlier stay in London, "it is as though you come from the dead. I heard of your return and am pleased to know that you did not die in the Reichenbach waters."

"And yet someone else just did, *nicht wahr?*" Holmes asked.

"*Ja,*" answered Steiler. "A young Englishman. Like you, from here he went walking on his own."

"It is his death, Herr Steiler, that we are here to investigate. How was he dressed?"

The old man thought for a moment, then smiled broadly as he remembered the details. "Heavy trousers. Heavy coat. Good boots. Flat cap."

Holmes nodded. "Nothing else?"

"But of course," said Steiler, "*schon vergessen.* A large rucksack he carried on his back."

"Ha!" cried Holmes, slapping his hand on the counter. "Precisely as I expected. Come, Watson. We shall soon get to the bottom of this mystery."

Snow-covered mountain peaks served as backdrop when for the second time in our adventures Holmes and I marched up the incline towards the series of falls. From the bottom of the road one cannot see the water itself, only the winding trail leading up and past the three mighty torrents that ultimately rain down as one. It took us some ten minutes to reach the lowest of the falls, an additional fifteen to reach the central, and another thirty to get to the uppermost.

Veiled in the shadows of the numerous fir trees, we plodded upward. Holmes kept his eyes on the ground searching for any tell-tale clues. For me, however, the path served only to conjure terrible memories. During that first ascent three years before, I had been called back to the hotel on a ruse; and I shall never forget the horrible fear I experienced when I rushed back up this same mountain trail hoping against hope that my friend still lived.

Now as then, the fearsome roar of the waterfall attracted us like a magnet. Skirting the ominous rock walls that towered above, I followed after Holmes in the direction of the thunderous din. To witness the waters cascade in waves of white foam down the glistening black walls of stone and plunge into the cavernous abyss is to see unmasked the overwhelming power and beauty of Nature.

Yet once we reached the narrow path leading to the edge of the final precipice, my morbid recollections eclipsed the grandeur. A wave of nausea overcame me as soon as I encountered the very boulder against which Holmes had leaned his Alpine stock and upon which he had left his farewell note. Enveloped by the clouds of mist and spray that hovered above the roiling waters, I forced myself to halt at a safe distance from the brink. The world around me was beginning to spin. With the mountain wall on one side and the straight drop a short distance before me, I placed my palm against the wet stone and took a series of deep breaths.

Holmes, who was stooping over a handful of black soil a few steps ahead, looked back over his shoulder and saw my condition. Whether my unsettled appearance affected his judgement, I shall never know, but with a quick shake of his head, he shouted at me over the water's roar, "No need to go any farther!" Then he gave the dirt in his hand a final peremptory look and tossed the stuff to the ground. "The path is of no use to us," said he loudly, slapping his hands together to rid them of any residual muck. "It's too moist, and too many footprints have already marred the trail. I should imagine that the authorities themselves have stomped across it and obliterated whatever clues we might have hoped to find."

"Are we done here, then?" I shouted back hopefully.

In answer, Holmes looked up at the sheer mountain wall by our side. "Do you see it, Watson?" he asked, pointing to a projection some twenty feet above our heads. "The ledge that shielded me when you brought the police here to examine the scene."

So long ago, and yet the memory of my exclusion from his plan still stings. I imagine that I will always harbour some resentment towards Holmes for letting me continue to think him dead. It was only the ultimate jubilation I experienced upon his return that alleviated the pain.

"We need another point of vantage," said he; and keeping his eye on the wall to our left, he proceeded to march back in the direction from which we had come. Though each step away from the edge helped restore my strength, I suddenly feared Holmes was searching for the invisible footholds he had employed in his earlier escape in order to scale the wall once again. At the point where the wall fell away, however, he stopped and, turning to his left once more, stared at a network of overgrown brambles and ferns.

"Aha!" he cried out at last and roughly pushed aside the overgrowth.

In an instant I perceived a hidden pathway ascending round the back of the mountain, and together Holmes and I scrambled up the steep terrain. Only when we reached a small plateau did I realise that we must be at the same spot where Colonel Moran had watched the struggle between Moriarty and Holmes unfold. It would have been here that

Moran, intent on completing the job that Moriarty had thankfully been unable to consummate, rained down upon Holmes a shower of large rocks and stones.

Today, of course, there were no such dangers. In spite of the tumble of tree branches that blocked a part of the view, we could now readily discern some twenty yards beneath us the rectangular outcropping that had served as Holmes's hiding place. The ledge was several feet deep; and verdant moss, like a green wool rug, blanketed the small nooks and crannies of its stone floor.

From an inner pocket, Sherlock Holmes drew a pair of binoculars, which he trained on the area below. "Owing to the proximity of the Falls," he observed as he peered through the lenses, "the moss-bed remains continuously moist. I can assure you from experience that not only does it provide a comfortable nest, but it also retains footmarks exceedingly well."

For a few moments more he proceeded to scan the ledge. "*Eureka!*" he suddenly shouted and, handing me the glasses, commanded, "Look for yourself."

I adjusted the lenses and observed the patterns in the moss more closely. Where before I had seen only gentle folds, I now made out among the rear shadows a long indentation where a body had recently lain. I could also begin to distinguish a few scattered footprints. At one edge of the projection, I detected what appeared to be the broad marks of a man's boots. At the other edge—

"Hold on," I said to Holmes. "Are those not the footprints of a woman's shoe?"

"Precisely what I expected," said Holmes, clapping his hands together.

"But what can such footprints mean? For that matter, Holmes, what does any of it mean?"

"To London, Watson," said he by way of answer. Motioning me to follow, he hurried along the downhill trail, his eyes focused on the path before him. Thanks to the information furnished by the binoculars, we now knew for what to look. And truth be told, clearly discernable along the way were the occasional woman's footprints mingling with all the other marks that had churned up much of the earth.

"We have learned all that we could hope for here in Switzerland," proclaimed Sherlock Holmes. "It is now time to reacquaint ourselves with Mr Reginald Bentley."

*****

Amberwell House, a modest building of soot-darkened stone, can be found in Southampton Row between Russell Square and Theobalds Road. Thanks to its proximity to the Inns of Court, the establishment provides lodgings for many of the solicitors and barristers who work nearby. Two days after our return from the Continent, Reginald Bentley suggested the Amberwell in response to our request to speak with him.

"Amberwell House at the end of my workday," he had wired back.

As he led us to a group of grey-leather-backed chairs in the corner of the small lobby, the moustached barrister seemed ill at ease. He continually looked round although, except for the clerk at the front desk and a man across the way hidden behind a newspaper, the lobby was deserted.

"We have just returned from the Reichenbach Falls, " Holmes began. "Let us get straight to the point, shall we?"

Avoiding Holmes's gaze, Bentley fidgeted with the cuffs of his jacket. "I don't know what you mean," he mumbled.

"We believe that your friend, Mr Leigh Smith-Mortimer, stole Dr Watson's notes that dealt with my near-death experience three years ago in Switzerland. As you previously confirmed with the map you showed us, just a few days later, you accompanied him in the re-creation of our previous trip. You alleged that he left you in your room at the *Englischer Hof* in order to go walking on his own. Further, you maintain that he never returned—that he fell, or hurled himself, to the bottom of the Falls."

"As I have already said."

"Then, sir," came Holmes's blunt reply, "not to put too fine a point on it, I do not believe you."

Bentley's eyes grew wide. He was about to sputter out some retort, but Holmes kept speaking.

"Oh, I do not doubt that Smith-Mortimer went off to the Falls on his own, but I must conclude that you knew of his plans from the start—that, in fact, the two of you conspired to make it appear that Leigh Smith-Mortimer had leaped to his death never to be heard from again."

"Now, see here, Mr Holmes," Bentley countered, "I won't have you disparage Leigh that way, not to mention myself. Do you not remember that it was I who notified the police?"

"And yet, Mr Bentley, it was also you who failed to inform them that the presumed-dead Smith-Mortimer was in reality hiding on the ledge not twenty feet above them when they investigated the scene. You must admit, sir, that—"
But Holmes never finished the sentence.

"Enough!" came the forceful, high-pitched voice of the man whom I supposed to have been reading the newspaper. He slammed the pages to the floor and stalked over to us. "Leave Reginald alone, Mr Holmes. *I* am the one you seek. I am Leigh Smith-Mortimer."

Holmes and I both stared up at the man—though, in truth, not very far up. From his photograph, we knew him to be shorter than his friend. But in the flesh, his entire stature appeared much slighter in spite of the Saville Row cut of his dark suit. His face bore delicate features, and his dark hair was trimmed short.

Reginald Bentley offered him his own seat while Bentley himself collected the chair that Smith-Mortimer had just been occupying.

"Well, well," Holmes said with a quick smile. "The very man we speak of. He who has dogged my footsteps to death's door at the Reichenbach Falls appears very much alive. What do you have to say for yourself, *sir*?" This last word was heavily emphasised, and at the same time there appeared in my friend's eye the same inexplicable twinkle that I had seen when he had first heard the details of the young man's disappearance.

"Reginald has told me," Leigh Smith-Mortimer replied, "that you already know how much I detest my father and his domination—all in the name of his legacy. A plague on that legacy! I tell you, Mr Holmes, that I could take it no longer. I wanted a means of escape. I've read of your investigations; and when I heard of your so-called death and resurrection, it gave me the idea to do the same.

"Your return being so recent, I assumed that Dr Watson would have his notes concerning the affair lying about. As you have surmised, I entered your rooms in disguise and stole his notebook. Reginald and I then followed all of your steps to be certain we didn't miss any of the planning that led to your success."

"Stealing my notes," I muttered. "Not very sporting."

"I'm sorry, Doctor, but your notebook furnished me with the kind of details I needed—like the footholds leading to the ledge above the path. As you did, Mr Holmes, I hid there from the police during their investigation; and when they had gone, I made my way back to London. Under a pseudonym, I took a room here at the Amberwell down the hall from Reginald. Now, I suppose, you will notify my father, and he will attempt to have me return to Windstone Hall."

"Your father is my client," said Holmes. "He has contracted me to find you. And yet, should I so choose, a rejection of his money would rid me of the responsibility."

The young man's eyes suddenly blazed with hope. "You'd do that, Mr Holmes?"

"I assure you, Mr Smith-Mortimer, that in the name of fair play, I have committed a number of unconventional actions. I am no official police force, you understand. But I must give your situation some thought. I don't overturn my clients' requests lightly. And whilst there is no law that will force you to go back to your father, the law of decency makes it imperative for me to let him know that you are alive and well. I suggest that we meet at Baker Street tomorrow afternoon. I shall send you a telegram once I have arranged the matter with Sir Lionel."

With that Holmes rose, and I followed. As we exited the Amberwell, I could not fail to notice that behind us an animated discussion was going on between the two young men.

*****

35

"Well, Watson, what do you make of the situation?" Holmes asked once we had found ourselves in Southampton Row again and walking towards the Strand.

"I believe that you were quite right in reserving additional time to consider your responsibilities. Still, I must say that there seems no let up in young Smith-Mortimer's grudge against his father. Unreasonable, I should think—in light of the rules that dictate the responsibilities of a titled son."

Sherlock Holmes stopped in his tracks. "Good old Watson—forever faithful to the traditions of our culture. And yet you miss the salient feature."

I could not see where Holmes was leading me. The antagonisms between father and son seemed quite clear.

"My dear fellow," said Holmes. "You have failed to recognise the fact that Mr Leigh Smith-Mortimer—'the titled son', as you call him—is in reality no son at all. He is, in fact, a woman."

Even I, the so-called man of words, was speechless. At last I spat out, "You—you can't be serious, Holmes."

"But I am, old fellow. Of course, you noted the delicate features, the smooth chin, the short but luxuriant hair, the small frame, the lilting voice."

"Yes, all of which proves nothing."

"But when you couple those decidedly feminine characteristics with a masculine life dictated by the unforgiving laws of primogeniture, you discover a wretched soul forced to play a part counter to her nature."

"But, Holmes. Surely birth certificates, doctors' statements—all would discount your inflammatory charges."

"Remember the birth, Watson. The couple were alone wandering the woods. Who knows? Perhaps Sir

Lionel had purposely arranged their isolated perambulations to coincide with the time the birth was expected. Fortunately, he himself managed to deliver the child; but unhappily, he could do nothing regarding the complications that killed Lady Smith-Mortimer. Clearly, there would be no more children. I imagine that in the confusion that followed, the doctors devoted their attention to saving the poor mother and simply taken Sir Reginald's word for the sex of the baby. Money paid out to wet-nurses and nannies would have purchased the silence of any others who knew the truth."

Such a wild plan certainly explained Holmes's fantastic accusation.

"I suspected some sort of ruse," said he, "as soon as Sir Lionel began complaining so bitterly about his son. I thought the old man protested too much. Upon observing the young person, I am now convinced."

"But the pretend suicide, Holmes, the climb up the mountain to the ledge. Surely, no *woman* could be expected to perform such feats!"

"Ah, Watson," Holmes smiled, "how did Hamlet put it to Horatio? 'There are more things in heaven and earth than are dreamt of in your philosophy.' I find women quite as capable as men in accomplishing whatever they put their mind to." He turned silent, and I knew he must have been thinking of the machinations set up by Irene Adler a few years before that had succeeded in thwarting Holmes himself.

"But what's the point?" I asked breaking into his thoughts. "Even if Sir Reginald had succeeded in passing the girl off as a boy, there could be no children in her future, no male heir to claim the estate."

"A crazed old man trying to hold on to what is his

for as long as possible," Holmes offered.   He grew silent again.   In fact, the only words he uttered after we had reached Aldwych, were, "Let us continue on to Simpson's. Afterwards, I shall make arrangements with Sir Lionel for tomorrow's meeting."

With the late-afternoon sun in our faces, we negotiated the Aldwych crescent, the walls of the buildings we passed casting shadows along the curve.   I remember thinking at the time how well those shadows epitomised the case.   Whatever had been going on in the mind of Sir Lionel Smith-Mortimer for the past twenty years must have been very murky indeed.

*****

Mrs Hudson had prepared tea for five people as we had requested.   The stooped form of Sir Lionel arrived first, his trek up our stairs again punctuated by the beat of his cane.   He looked at the tea service and chocolate biscuits set out on the dining table, shook his head, and selected an armchair to sit upon that was far removed from the table.

"Tell me your news, Holmes," he demanded.

"In due time, sir.   We await the others."

"What others?"

As if in answer, a sharp knock rattled our door. Holmes opened it to Reginald Bentley.   The barrister entered the room, but not by himself.   He was accompanied by a magnificent young woman in a dress of yellow cotton, accented in white at the neck and cuffs.   Adorned with a white feather, a small yellow hat was perched coquettishly upon her short black curls.   It nearly took my breath away to realise that only the day before I had been conversing with

38

this very person under the impression that I was speaking to one Leigh Smith-Mortimer, the only son of a Baronet.

"Watson," said Holmes with a gesture towards the lady, "may I re-introduce you to Leigh Smith-Mortimer. That is, *Miss* Leigh Smith-Mortimer."

"Now see here!" interrupted Sir Lionel. "I won't stand for this *charade*."

Miss Smith-Mortimer had been about to take my hand when she wheeled upon her father. "*You* won't stand for this *charade*?" she charged, cheeks reddening, nostrils flaring. "I've been play-acting in your little game for as long as I can remember. Always the boy—to preserve the line! Even though you've always known that the line would end with me. You knew I could never marry as a man. And now I have found someone who has seen through this masquerade and wants to love me as a woman should be loved. I am through with your game, Father. May Windstone Hall crumble to the earth for all I care!"

"Leigh," Sir Lionel said, holding out both hands. "After your mother died and there was no possibility for a male heir—"

"Stop, Father!" she cried. "I have heard all this nonsense before. Let the succession fall to cousins twice-removed—or *three*-times removed. I don't care! It doesn't matter any more. You robbed me of my proper childhood, and I won't allow you to rob me of my marriage." She turned to Bentley. "That is," she said, her voice now lowered, "if you'll have me."

Reginald Bentley took her in his arms. "I love you, Leigh. Your beautiful nature has always shone through your disguise. We did our best to kill off the male version of yourself; and now, thanks to Mr Holmes, you've been able to speak the truth."

The young woman stood as tall as she could. "I am leaving you now, Father," she said simply. "As you've just heard, Reginald and I will soon be married. Good man that he is, he has convinced me to invite you to the wedding. It is your choice whether you want to gain a daughter and, God willing, grandchildren or live on in isolation. The choice will be yours."

Before leaving, the couple turned to Holmes and me. "Thank you, gentlemen," said Bentley. "At first I feared you might bring ruination upon us, but now I see that shining a light on this bizarre story has instead brought us salvation." The two of them smiled and hand in hand slowly made their way down the stairs.

With a dissatisfied grunt, Sir Lionel leaned on his cane in order to stand. He took a deep breath and, without looking at either Holmes or me, placed a one-hundred-pound note on the table as he shuffled to the door.

No one uttered a word. Once the door closed, I walked to the table set for tea and sampled one of Mrs Hudson's chocolate biscuits.

*****

Reginald Bentley had relatives who lived in the hamlet of Icomb in Gloucestershire   It was there in the tiny church of St. Mary the Virgin a few short weeks after the events described that he and Leigh Smith-Mortimer chose to marry. Holmes and I were invited to the ceremony, but we decided not to attend. It was to be a small affair, and our presence would only serve to raise uncomfortable questions. Happily, there were no pressmen in attendance, and Miss

Smith-Mortimer sent us an account in her own hand of all that had transpired.

True to her word, she did request her father's presence. And I am pleased to report that, difficult as it was for the old man both physically and emotionally, Sir Lionel travelled to Gloucestershire to give his daughter away. Villagers must have wondered about the splendid carriage and liveried footman at so simple a ceremony, but their wonder never reached the spiteful arena of London gossip— at least not then.

It would take three years and the death of Sir Lionel for the facts regarding his mistreatment of his daughter to become the fodder of scandal throughout the land. Just as the Baronet had predicted, with no son to inherit the estate, the grand manor house along with the rest of the riches was passed on by virtue of entailment to a distant Canadian cousin called Randolph Carlton Smith.

It had been my desire to maintain the privacy of the newly-married couple. To that end, I included the Smith-Mortimer affair in the collection of cases from 1894 that I chose not to make public. Yet however noble in intent, the gesture turned out to be laughably feeble.

Periodicals could not print enough about the story to satisfy the public. Newspapers constantly rehashed the details; magazines furnished long-winded biographies of the principals. So widespread were the accounts of the ugly business that one can understand why I had originally referred to the entailment case as "famous". In retrospect, I believe that "infamous" would have been the more appropriate adjective.

Capitol Murder

For an educated human being to arrange an assassination,
he must have a streak of the monster in him—
even if the man he purposes to be slain
is regarded by him and by multitudes
as an enemy of God and man.

--David Graham Phillips
"The Assassination
of a Governor"
The Cosmopolitan, April 1905

I

I suppose that the appearance of yet another American should not have been surprising. After all, a great many of them have played significant roles in some of the most celebrated adventures of my friend and colleague Mr Sherlock Holmes. Why, our very first investigation together, the case I titled *A Study in Scarlet*, involved the American Jefferson Hope and the Mormons of Utah. And Holmes himself will never forget Miss Irene Adler of New Jersey, the female adversary whose successes earned from him the distinctive accolade of "*the* woman". For that matter, I myself was shot in the leg by one James Winter, the notorious "Killer" Evans from Chicago.

I might also add that my literary agent, Arthur Conan Doyle, who knows a thing or two about successful publishing, has always encouraged me to promote the American angle. "It's good for business, Watson," he constantly reminds me. "Sprinkling your adventures with Americans broadens the market." How else to interpret Sir Arthur's delight upon meeting William Gillette, the American actor famous for depicting Holmes on stage, and who at the time of the encounter was fully dressed in ear-flapped travelling cap and long grey coat?

According to the reports, Gillette approached Sir Arthur with magnifying glass in hand and, after examining him closely, proclaimed, "Unquestionably an author!"

Though it would be a few years before I personally witnessed Gillette's impersonation of Holmes, I was never convinced by it. Not only did I not see the resemblance, but I could also not forget that it was Gillette who popularised for the entire world the inaccurate notion that Holmes smoked a calabash pipe and always donned a deerstalker.

There was simply no need for false *accoutrements*. With so many English trappings already associated with the man—the Baker Street address, the London backdrop, *Bradshaw's Railway Guide* (not to mention his generally stoic nature)—Sherlock Holmes fully epitomised the British character. He required no help from the Americans.

Yet in spite of such misinformation that appeared in the United States, I continue to marvel at the large number of Holmes's investigations that truly did have connections to America. One need only glance at some of our most celebrated adventures to discover just how much of Holmes's career depended upon cases linked to the States.

These cases include (to name but a few): "The Noble Bachelor" featuring the ill-fated marriage of Hattie Doran from San Francisco; "The Problem of Thor Bridge" dealing with a former American Senator; and "The Dancing

Men" involving the peculiar stick-figure code employed by American gangsters. Two cases, "The Five Orange Pips" and "The Yellow Face", suggested the pernicious effects of Southern prejudice; and in "His Last Bow", Holmes himself assumed the role of an England-hating Irish-American before the onset of the Great War. One must also not forget two other cases, "The Red Circle" and *The Valley of Fear*, that brought within Holmes's professional circle Agents Leverton and Edwards, a pair of investigators from Pinkerton, the renowned American detective agency.

There is, however, a hitherto unknown investigation linked to this same Birdy Edwards that involves yet a third Pinkerton operator. Though much less dramatic than Edwards's clandestine work in Pennsylvania's Vermissa Valley, equally significant was the simple act he performed in referring a colleague to our Baker Street rooms.

In point of fact, it was this innocent recommendation that led to the conclusion of a political drama containing one of the most cold-blooded operations Holmes ever undertook. The less charitable among us might even say that the adventure I publish here for the first time lays at the feet of the world's first consulting detective the indisputable charge of premeditated murder.

*****

The origins of the ugly business occurred in the middle of a wintry morning in late February of 1900. Holmes and I sat warming ourselves by the fire when Billy the page brought to our rooms a tall, thin, clean-shaven gentleman with a strong, square jawline. He wore a long black coat over a dark suit, white shirt, bowstring tie, and stovepipe trousers. Square-toed Western boots peeked out at the cuff, and his left hand was holding what appeared to be a dark-brown, wide-brimmed Stetson hat with a flattened crown. One did not need to hear him speak to conclude that yet another American was about to make his presence known.

"Wyatt Steele, Mr Holmes," said our visitor, extending his hand. "I'm a Pinkerton agent." His flat intonations confirmed his provenance.

Holmes offered his own hand and then introduced me.

"Glad to meet you, Dr Watson," said Steele, gripping my hand with an air of confidence. He appeared to be in his mid-thirties, and I must admit that he cut quite a figure, every bit the straight-backed American that the Pinkertons had the reputation for hiring.

"I know it was a few years ago, Mr Holmes," he went on, "but if you recall my old pal Birdy Edwards, he was the one who said to look you up if I ever needed help in London. He wrote a quick note to me before he vacated Birlstone Manor. It was right after you investigated a murder there. He didn't sign the letter, but I knew it was from Birdy all the same."

Sherlock Holmes smiled. "I do indeed remember Mr Edwards, a fearless Irishman with a singular mind. Lost at sea a few years back—or so the story runs—presumably, another victim of the late and unlamented Professor Moriarty." The smile waned as he contemplated the destructive power of his former enemy.

"Hold on," said Steele, raising his hat as a kind of stop-sign, "I had no intention of setting off so dark a mood. To tell you the truth," he announced, "I'm actually here on Pinkerton business."

Holmes took the man's hat and coat and hung them on a peg near the still-open door. Then, indicating to our guest a cushioned chair near the fire, he proceeded to shout down the stairwell at the page-boy. "Billy!" he cried. "Ask Mrs Hudson to send up tea—on second thought, make it coffee in honour of our American friend."

I heard a murmur of what sounded like assent from below before Holmes closed the door and joined me in his own armchair opposite our guest.

"Now, Mr Steele," said Holmes, "pray, tell us what sort of Pinkerton business has caused you to seek me out on so miserable a day. Other than the assassination of Kentucky's governor a few weeks ago, I recall no other recent crimes in America that might have caused you to come all this way."

Steele's mouth gaped wide. For a moment, the calm and cool Pinkerton agent seemed to have lost his composure. "Wh—how? How did you know?" he stammered.

I shared his amazement. Holmes's words were the first I had heard of any such affair.

"The newspapers provide all sorts of information," he said with the wave of his hand. "And when it comes to more vital issues of state, my brother Mycroft also keeps me informed."

"However you've come by the news, Mr Holmes, you're quite correct. I am indeed on the trail of the killer of William Goebel, the short-lived governor of Kentucky. He was shot in Frankfort, the state's capital; and I have good reason to believe his assassin has come to London. But then you seem to know much of this already."

"I make it my business to keep abreast of a variety of crimes, Mr Steele, though I must confess that political assassinations generally fail to interest me. They're too prosaic. One politician doesn't like another and—bang!" Holmes pointed his long index finger like a gun at Steele and pretended to fire. "Motives are obvious, and means are generally unimaginative. Not much to hold my attention, I'm afraid. This case, however, features some curious echoes."

I had participated in most of Holmes's investigations, yet I remained at a loss regarding the so-called "echoes" to which he alluded.

"Allow me to tell you what I know about the case," offered Steele. "Perhaps we might then combine our knowledge and reach some sort of conclusion. It's the sort of thing Birdy said you were so good at."

Just then Mrs Hudson arrived with Billy in tow. He was holding a tray with her silver service and a few biscuits neatly arranged on a large plate. Mrs Hudson herself placed the fixings on the low table near our guest, filled our cups with coffee, observed that all was in order, and only then— with a brief dip of her head—fairly pushed Billy out the door ahead of her.

Whilst we listened to the two of them thumping down the stairs, Holmes leaned forward to sample the coffee. Finding it to his satisfaction, he placed his cup back on its saucer and turned to our guest. "Now, Mr Steele, pray tell us about this unfortunate William Goebel. What had he done to bring about his death; and, for that matter, what is there about his murder that is mysterious enough to have engaged the likes of the Pinkertons?"

As if to fortify himself, the American drank some of his coffee. Thus prepared, he began his tale. "First, one must understand William Goebel the man. Ironically for a politician, he wasn't a particularly likeable fellow—at least, according to those who knew him. Not many people were close to him. Besides his brothers and sister, he seemed to have few friends. There were no women in his life besides his sister; and while he advocated reforms for working people, most folks believed that it was their votes he sought rather than their true well-being."

I grunted in agreement. I could name many a duplicitous politician in England who fit the same bill.

"Nor was Goebel much of a speaker," said Steele. "I'd been to one of his political rallies when I was travelling through Frankfort. Oh, he'd go through the motions, but his words didn't soar. You'd have to turn elsewhere—to someone like William Jennings Bryan, who had, in fact, campaigned for him—if you wanted to get your blood flowing. Goebel's looks weren't much to speak of either. He had pale skin, narrow eyes, and plastered-down, black hair. To tell the truth, there was something reptilian about him."

Holmes and I exchanged glances. I knew that we were harbouring the same suspicions. Holmes had once compared the ruthless blackmailer, Charles Augustus Milverton, to a serpent, but the only person I had ever heard Holmes specifically describe as "reptilian" was the cold-blooded Moriarty himself.

"And yet despite such obstacles," continued the American, "Goebel successfully climbed the political ladder. In the name of the common people, he stood up to the L & N—that's the Louisville and Nashville railroad—the major line in Kentucky. He called them 'blood-suckers', said their labour practices were unfair, their ticket prices too high, their interests only concerned with financial gain. It was a good sales pitch all right, and he rode it straight to the leadership of Kentucky's Democratic Party. He became quite the power broker. People called him czar, King Goebel, even William the Conqueror."

"One presumes," observed Holmes quietly, "that in the process he also collected some formidable enemies—the so-called L & N in particular."

"Precisely, Mr Holmes. It was, in fact, the leadership of the L & N—Basil Duke and Milton Smith, to be precise—that hired Pinkerton to find out who killed Goebel. They want L & N's name cleared. You see, as Goebel's principal adversaries, they fear being held responsible for the assassination themselves—as by some, I can assure you, they already are. There are plenty of Kentucky Democrats who'd think nothing of shooting a likely suspect—especially if he runs a railroad."

"So I have read," said Holmes. "No, offense, Mr Steele, but even before this latest outrage, a number of pressmen have already referred to Kentucky as the most violent state in your country."

"No offense taken, Mr Holmes." With a chuckle, he added, "I'm from Montana," and proceeded to revisit his coffee.

"Kentucky's a dangerous place all right," he went on. "They have their own methods for working things out. It's funny. Though Goebel wasn't born there either, he seemed to fit right in. A while back, he had a dispute with a banker named Sanford. Planned or not, they happened to meet out on the street. Within seconds, guns were drawn, shots were fired, and Goebel's bullet struck Sanford in the head. The man died not long thereafter. That's how they take care of things in Kentucky."

Frontier justice, I could not help thinking. To the average Englishman, myself included, Kentucky seemed no different from the rest of that lawless country.

"Which," continued Steele, "brings us back to that fateful day last month when Goebel was shot. The election for governor took place in early November."

"The election presumably won by Goebel," I noted. "You already told us he was the governor."

"If it only were that simple, Doctor. A Republican named William Taylor—'Hogjaw' Taylor, they call him— came out ahead and was actually inaugurated in December; but, you see, Goebel had previously set up his own legislative committee to rule on the integrity of the election, and he appealed to them in hopes of having the results reversed.

"Yet much to everyone's surprise—especially Goebel's—his handpicked committee confirmed Taylor's victory. Goebel still had another card to play, however; and he appealed the committee's decision to his allies in the heavily Democratic state legislature. In fact, it was when Goebel was on his way to hear the final deliberations that he was cut down. It was only *after* he was shot that the Democratic legislature overturned the election results and declared Goebel the new governor. Mortally wounded— some say he was already dead—he was sworn in the next day, the 31st of January 1900. He died three days later."

"My word," said I. "Quite a dramatic tale."

Holmes leaned back in his chair, steepled his fingers, and closed his eyes. "Describe the scene of the shooting, if you please, Mr Steele."

"With your permission," said the American, withdrawing a small pocketbook from inside his coat. He flipped through a few pages to consult his notes and then reported the following: "On the morning of Tuesday, January 30—a cold, crisp day it was—Goebel set off with two friends for the state house from the Capital Hotel where he was staying. It was just a short walk—one block down Main Street and up St. Clair to Broadway.

"You must understand that due to the contested election, feelings were running high. This was Kentucky, after all; and most of Frankfort seemed an armed camp. Mountaineers from the south-eastern counties that supported Taylor—some called them '*desperadoes*'—roamed the streets with pistols, rifles, and shotguns—presumably with the intent of intimidating the legislature into supporting Taylor. For their part, the Democrats responded with newly-sworn-in police to help maintain the peace. With all the talk of violence, of course, it was feared that somebody might eventually try to shoot Goebel himself.

"Which is why those two friends who accompanied Goebel to the Capitol that morning also served as bodyguards. At first, it seemed they weren't needed; for when the three arrived at Capitol Square, they found the area—it's a full city block—almost completely deserted."

"The scene, Mr Steele," Holmes repeated, eyes still closed. "Describe the scene."

Steele nodded. "The grounds themselves are pretty flat, interrupted here and there this time of year by barren hackberry trees. The square is surrounded by an iron-rail fence. That morning, a thin layer of snow covered the ground. The water in the four-tiered fountain near the Capitol's steps had frozen. The Capitol building itself, a two-storey, brick and white-stone structure, stands at the centre of the square. It's one of those places in the Greek revival style and has a portico with six large columns that hold up the gabled pediment."

Sherlock Holmes opened his eyes at the preciseness of the description. "Six columns you say?"

"I know what you're thinking, Mr Holmes," said Steele. "An assassin hidden behind one of those columns could do some damage. But, you see, a shooter in the portico would be easily detected; there isn't enough cover. The front of the building contains no windows and only a single entrance."

Holmes nodded, and the fire crackled in accompaniment.

"At 11.16," Steele continued, "Goebel and his two bodyguards made a turn into the square through one of the two open gates and proceeded up the wide stone walkway. No doubt you could have heard their shoes crunching the leftover snow on the pavement. It's about a hundred feet from the street to the portico, and the walkway itself inclines slightly as you approach the building. One of the bodyguards went ahead to check that the interior was safe; the other dropped back a step or two.

"It was just then—right before Goebel reached the fountain—that shots rang out. Some say Goebel tried to draw his own pistol; but the wound was too great, and he fell to the ground. 'Get me away,' he's said to have uttered, 'I'm afraid it's all over for me.'"

"How many shots?" Holmes asked.

"Not certain. Maybe five. Maybe fewer. There were too many conflicting accounts. Needless to say, the assassin escaped, identity unknown."

"Of course," said Holmes. "A situation you plan to rectify."

"One may hope," Steele replied. "But what I *can* tell you with certainty is that a single bullet traveling downward pierced Goebel's right side; splintered a rib; passed through a lung; and exited his back. He was carried to his hotel room; and doctors were summoned. But ultimately, the damage was too great.

"A few days later, after having been sworn in as governor and visited by his sister and one of his brothers—the other couldn't get there in time—Goebel died. I suppose it's fitting that controversy dogs his last words. Democrats say that he told his friends to 'be brave, fearless, and loyal to the great common people.'"

"Quite noble in the end," I observed. "A confirmation of the man's social concerns."

"To be sure," said Steele, "if true. One of his doctors reported that his final words were in fact a complaint about his last meal. 'Damned bad oyster,' he's supposed to have said."

I shook my head in disbelief and changed the subject. "What did the police make of all this? Surely their investigation must have turned up some valuable information."

Steele allowed himself another short laugh. "Well, Doctor," he drawled, "at least I can't say they didn't try. They did determine that a rifle had been fired from a window in the next-door Executive Building. It's a three-storey brick structure some forty feet to the east of the Capitol."

"You said 'from *a* window', Mr Steele," Holmes pointed out. "Not from *the* window?"

"Good point, Mr Holmes. Exactly *which* window wasn't so easy to identify. Remember that there were just a handful of people walking around at the time. A few of them pointed at the nearest open window. It was in the southwest corner of the Executive Building—which, incidentally, just happened to be the private office of the newly-elected Secretary of State, a Republican named Caleb

Powers. The shade was down most of the way, and the window was raised about six inches."

"There you have it," said I.

"Not quite, Doctor. You see, a number of other people maintained that the shot had actually come from higher up. A few said they'd actually seen a rifle barrel in a third-floor window."

"Certainly," said Holmes, "an immediate investigation would turn up the appropriate evidence to establish the facts."

Now anyone familiar with the investigative methods of Sherlock Holmes could predict that, had Holmes been there himself, he would have invaded the offices on both floors, fallen to his hands and knees in each, and begun peering through his glass in search of vital clues.

"So one would assume, Mr Holmes. So one would assume." Here Steele paused—almost as if to draw keener attention to his next few words.

Holmes did, in fact, lean forward. "I sense that you're suggesting some impediment to the investigation."

Steele laughed again. "Indeed I am," said he. "You see, Bill Taylor, the soon-to-be *deposed* Kentucky governor, had been paralyzed by fear even before Goebel' shooting. And with good reason. Upon the arrival of Taylor's mountain men, Goebel's people had begun marching around with guns.

"The assault on their Democratic leader brought matters to a boil; and seething with anger they screamed about killing the Republican Taylor. Fearing for his own safety, not to mention that of his family, Taylor had no hesitation in ordering in the state militia. Within minutes of the shooting, five-hundred strong of the Louisville Legion and the 2d Regiment filled the square. Their bayonets at the ready, the fully uniformed militiamen stood positioned to prevent anyone from entering the area—which obviously included the scene of the crime. *'Anyone'*, of course, meant the police as well."

"Preposterous!" I exploded. The thought of soldiers hindering a criminal investigation—let alone blocking the state's elected representatives from convening in the Capitol building—seemed unworthy of a democratic nation.

Steele merely shrugged. "As you could have predicted, the local authorities got no help at all from the Republicans. In fact, to the best of my knowledge, Taylor and his crew are still holed up in the Executive Building. By my count, it's been some three weeks now. Taylor told the Republican legislators to meet in the town of London— London, Kentucky, that is; and the Democrats are gathering in the Capital Hotel in Frankfort. It's like the state has two governments."

Holmes offered a single, sarcastic clap of his hands. "Wonderful!" he cried, "a regular comedy of errors."

"Don't get me wrong, Mr Holmes," countered Steele. "Plenty of arrests were made. In fact, some twenty-seven people were rounded up at the start—clerks, politicians, even a state-police officer. But from what I've been hearing lately, suspicion has focused on three: Caleb Powers, the Republican Secretary of State—"

"From whose office the bullet was fired," I interrupted.

"*Might* have been fired, Doctor," Steele corrected. "Powers was thought to be the mastermind. A stenographer and notary public named Henry Youtsey, was charged with being the go-between. He worked in the state auditor's office just down the hall from Powers. Youtsey's the one they think hid a pair of rifles—a Marlin .38-55 and a

Winchester .38-56—behind a loose wooden plank in Powers's office. The last of the three, a Republican county assessor named Jim Howard, had previously been charged with some other murder. Apparently, *he* is now considered the gunman. I should add that Powers himself had conveniently arranged to be out of town at the time of the shooting."

Holmes nodded. "It sounds like the authorities have constructed a logical case, Mr Steele. But you still seem to harbour doubts?"

"I do, Mr Holmes—to a point. All these charges against Powers and the others may, in fact, be true; but I have to believe there's more. A full ten days after the shooting, the police discovered a .38 calibre bullet in the trunk of a hackberry tree not far behind where Goebel had been hit. The bullet matched one of the rifles found in Powers's office. As a consequence, the police employed an engineer to show that one end of a taut string held at the bullet hole in the tree and the other end at Powers's corner-window would have passed directly through the point where Goebel had been standing, thus proving the origin of the shot."

"One moment," said Holmes. "How high was the bullet hole in the tree?"

"About four-and-a-half feet from the ground."

"And the distance between the ground and the bottom of Powers's window?"

"About the same."

"Hah!" Holmes cried. "Earlier you said that the bullet which struck Goebel had travelled *downward.*"

"Exactly." Steele grinned. "You're an excellent listener, Mr Holmes. What's more, you're also giving voice to the same thoughts I have."

Sherlock Holmes cocked an eyebrow.

"You see, I couldn't forget the witnesses—more than a dozen, actually—who'd mentioned a third-floor window. They all agreed the shots had come from somewhere between the Capitol and the office building, which I took to mean from the office building's west side, not from a front-corner window like Powers's. For that matter, I'm told that Howard, the alleged shooter, didn't seem a calm enough type to have lain in wait and done the deed. Oh, some people did swear they'd seen him on the Capitol grounds near the time of the shooting, but he produced his own witnesses to say he was elsewhere.

"Assuming you're the sort of investigator I perceive you to be," said Holmes, "I imagine that you tried to confirm your doubts."

Steele smiled again. "On the second day of the occupation by the militia, I was able to check that third-floor office myself. I bribed one of the men—$20 of L & N money was quite a sum to convince him to lend me his uniform for an hour or two."

"Excellent!" cried Holmes.

"Disguised as a soldier, I entered the Executive Building, climbed the stairs, and visited the room in question."

"What did you find?" Holmes asked, his grey eyes blazing.

"The room itself had been swept clean. And yet in front of the window stood two boxes, one on top of the other, reaching to the level of the windowsill. Need I say, a perfect place to rest a rifle? But there's more. The wooden floor revealed scuffmarks in front of the boxes that suggested a person had been moving around at that spot.

And that's not all. You see, there was something strange about the markings."

"Strange?" Holmes repeated. "In what manner were they 'strange'?"

Steele consulted his notes again. "Most were long, sweeps—as if a foot had been dragged along the floor rather than simply having stepped upon it—as if whoever made the marks had a bad leg."

"Well done, Mr Steele!" cried Holmes. "At long last. Anything else?"

"One more thing, Mr Holmes. I found *this!* It must have been brushed into a corner.*" As he spoke, he drew from inside his coat a long, white envelope, which he handed to my friend.

Like a starving man reaching for food, Holmes shot out his hand to receive it. Carefully opening the flap, he slowly drew from the envelope what looked to be a short, metal rod. It had a small wooden handle at one end and a tiny, round, bolt-like device at the other. Only after scrutinizing the entire piece, did he roll the thing between his thumb and forefinger.

"*Ein Hebel,*" he murmured.

"What's that, Holmes?" I asked.

"*Hebel* is German for lever."

"You recognise it then?" asked Steele. "I figured it must be important, but I didn't know what it was."

"It is the lever," Holmes said, holding the rod vertically so Steele and I could examine it as he spoke, "used for priming the bellows within an air rifle. You'll remember, Watson, that back in '94 Sebastian Moran employed such a weapon (what the Germans call a *Bolzenbüchse*) for shooting at me—though in Moran's case, it had been modified by that tinker von Herder. I told you that this case offered familiar echoes."

Who could forget the horrible night when the dummy-likeness of Holmes that he had placed in our Baker Street window had taken the bullet meant for the man himself? It seemed like yesterday though almost six years had passed.

"If I understand you correctly," Wyatt Steele addressed my friend, "you're suggesting that the assassin was, in fact, at the third-floor window of the Executive Building with an air-rifle."

"Quite so. I shouldn't doubt that, as you yourself have described, there were also shooters in the office of the Secretary of State. Let's not forget that there were gunmen running rampant throughout the city. Still, I'm willing to wager that the shooters in Powers's office were meant to be diversions. Oh, I have no doubt that they fired upon Goebel—one even hit a tree!—but whoever wanted him dead had put his true faith in the shooter with the silent weapon on the third floor. He's the gunman we're really after."

"A gunman with a gamy leg," I said.

"Exactly, Watson. And unless I am very much mistaken, I believe it is the same conclusion that has compelled Mr Steele to continue his investigation.

"Indeed, Mr Holmes. But not with the assuredness that your confirmation provides. While I was still in uniform, I asked some of the soldiers nearby if they'd seen anyone limping about."

"And?"

"'Now that you mention it,' said one, 'I do remember a beggar hanging around. A cripple he was. He had a bad back and twisted leg. He was wearing a pea coat and bell-bottomed trousers—you know, the kind that sailors wear. I remember his sea-faring clothes because I thought they looked pretty strange out here in the middle of Kentuck.'

"'And another thing,' a second soldier chimed in, 'even though he looked young, he walked with a cane. I guess 'cause he was all hunched over.''

"A walking stick, Watson," said Holmes. "Do you mark that?"

I did though I failed to make anything of it. That a deformed man required a walking stick did not seem unusual to me.

"Where was he seen?" Holmes asked.

"On Broadway in front of the Capitol grounds. Apparently, he was holding out a tin cup for money; but in all the commotion, he started hobbling east towards Ann Street. You should know, Mr Holmes, that just past the corner of the square is the L & N railroad depot. It's quite close by actually—only a couple of blocks away. Once I got back into my regular clothes, I checked there myself. A ticket agent told me he'd seen a cripple begging out in Elk Alley next to the station. As far as I could tell, no one actually saw him get on a train, but you know how it is— once word gets around about a shooting, people start running every which way. I don't imagine they'd pay any mind to a beggar, not even a deformed one."

"You're suggesting," I said to Steele, "that this cripple boarded a train at the railway station and got out of town."

"I am," said the Pinkerton agent. "And depending on time and destination, he could have made connections to most anywhere. Say he got to Cincinnati. Then he could travel north. "

"Or west," I suggested, images of frontier gunslingers springing to mind.

"I wagered on New York," offered Steele. "The pea coat and flared trousers made me think of a seaport—a place where he could fit in—and New York is the major point of departure—"

"—For ships sailing to almost anywhere," said Holmes, completing the sentence.

"I figured it was worth looking into. I notified the agency to get some people out to the New York docks and keep an eye peeled for the twisted man."

"Excellent work, Mr Steele," said Holmes. "I can only assume that someone saw him board a ship for London, which is why you are here."

"That's right. The Pinkerton Agency has had many dealings with the Metropolitan Police, and I cabled Scotland Yard to be on the lookout at the London docks for the suspect. An Inspector Lestrade was put in charge, but I guess that the crippled man somehow managed to elude him."

"Fancy that," said Holmes drily, "a crippled man eluding Lestrade." He allowed himself a brief chuckle and then said to the two of us, "Well, gentlemen, I suppose it will be up to us to track down the fugitive."

Steele's eyes widened. "Do you actually have someone in mind, Mr Holmes?"

"By itself, I grant you that the naval attire doesn't tell us much. But when I match it to a deformed young man with the intent to kill, a certain profile most certainly comes to mind. What say *you*, friend Watson?"

There was indeed a ring of familiarity in the description, yet I could not place the figure in question.

"And if I tell you," Holmes said to me, "that a trip to Sussex might be in order—to Cheeseman's in Lamberley just south of Horsham?"

"Bob Ferguson!" I cried.

"More properly, Bob Ferguson's son, Master Jacky."

Steele knotted his eyebrows. His confusion could well be understood since I had not yet made public the case I intended to title "The Sussex Vampire". The narrative would dramatise for the reading public the young man to whom Holmes was referring.

"Jacky Ferguson is the son of an old friend of mine," I explained. "In our rugby days, the boy's father was known as 'Big Bob'."

Holmes cleared his throat to remind me to stick to the salient facts.

"By 1896," I continued, "Bob's wife—that is to say, Jacky's mother—had died, Fergusson remarried, and soon they had a new son."

"Not long thereafter," said Holmes, "the trouble started."

"In November of that year," I told Steele, "Ferguson came to Holmes seeking an explanation for the apparently murderous intentions of his second wife towards the baby. As it turned out, however, it was not Bob's wife but the pampered older boy Jacky—I called him *boy*, he must be close to twenty by now—who had attempted to poison his tiny half-brother. His was a decidedly murderous plan intended to prevent the baby from coming between himself and his father. After revealing the crime, Holmes suggested to Ferguson that his son spend a year at sea."

The Pinkerton agent furrowed his brow. "I don't understand how—"

"Sorry," I said. "I failed to mention that the boy Jacky had suffered a terrible fall during his childhood. The result was—"

"Let me guess," Steele interrupted. "A twisted spine."

"Quite so," said Holmes. "Now, Watson, wire Ferguson with the news that we're coming to visit. We can catch an afternoon train at Victoria. No need to mention Master Jacky until we actually get there. Mr Steele, I'm afraid we'll have to leave you to your own devices until we return. Three people descending on poor Robert Ferguson would be too many."

"Whatever you say, Mr Holmes. I'm in your hands. I never expected to have identified a suspect so quickly. Birdy Edwards certainly had you pegged correctly."

A brief smile flashed across Holmes's face. He was never one to ignore a compliment.

II

As Sherlock Holmes had proposed, he and I took the afternoon train from Victoria to Horsham. Though ashen clouds and a lingering February chill attempted to bedevil the Sussex landscape, hosts of golden daffodils, wild red clover, white snowdrops, and pink camellias maintained the beauty of the picturesque countryside.

Yet I had no desire to gaze out the carriage window. On the contrary, I preferred to fasten my eyes on Holmes as he revealed to me the various actions that had been going on directly under my nose but about which I clearly knew nothing.

"Surely, Watson, once we discovered Master Jacky's vile role in that vampire business, you didn't imagine I'd let him go off in the world unobserved? One doesn't expect a sour temper to sweeten overnight. That is why I requested your friend Ferguson to notify me as soon as he secured a ship's berth for the boy. It took a few weeks; but the shipping agents at Ferguson's firm, tea brokers Ferguson and Muirhead of Mincing Lane, were finally able to complete the assignment. A position 'before the mast', as it were, was established for young Jack on the *S.S Heraldic*, a tea-carrying steamer in the Merchant Navy. What's more, from all reports, the boy appeared ready, if a bit reluctant, to perform his shipboard tasks to the extent that his physical abilities allowed.

"Most admirable," I said, pleased that my friend's son seemed to be falling into line.

"And yet, Watson, I needed to be certain. No sooner did I learn that Jacky would be setting out to sea from Gravesend than I put Sammy Trout and the other Baker Street Irregulars on his scent. With comrades all along the river, I knew that the Irregulars would have little difficulty keeping track of a flaxen-haired youth that exhibited a decided limp. I instructed Sam to inform me when they actually saw him boarding.

"Once Jacky had set sail, it was a simple matter to chart the *Heraldic*'s comings and goings in the newspapers' recordings of commercial ship movements. My various contacts in European and American ports served to confirm what I had already learned, and such has been the case for the past three years."

Three years! —During which time *I* had suspected nothing. The railway carriage swayed back and forth, and under ordinary circumstances the movement might have lulled me to sleep. But on this occasion, so annoyed was I at having not been told about what was going on with the son of my old friend that drowsiness never threatened.

"How did young Jack fare as a sailor then?" I asked.

"As one might expect, Watson," said Holmes, unsurprisingly oblivious to my annoyance. "The boy viewed anything required of him as punishment. Let us not forget that Master Jacky regarded his attempts to kill the baby as perfectly logical. As a result, his exile to shipboard labour must have seemed very unjust punishment indeed."

"And yet a moment ago you described him as resigned to facing his sea adventure."

"Ah, Watson," Holmes sighed, "I'm afraid it only gets worse. As a not-too surprising consequence, the boy began to cultivate undesirable associates among his shipmates. One imagines that it took little effort on their part to interest the bitter young man in firearms, and Jack soon extended his so-called 'tour of duty' aboard the *Heraldic*. Guns, you see, made no demands on his deformity—indeed, here were weapons that allowed him to gain the strength that he'd always felt he was lacking."

"Surely, Holmes, you didn't learn all this from the Baker Street Irregulars? Good watchdogs, so to speak, but mere children lacking the psychological insights you are reporting."

"Hah, Watson! Sharp as ever. No, the Irregulars merely presented the facts; I supplied the inferences. As it turned out, Jack had returned to Gravesend with an unsavoury group of friends. One of our lads followed them to the marshlands outside of town and watched them shoot at bottles and the like. Jack, it seems, had become quite proficient.

"Once I heard that he'd begun taking aim at stray dogs and cats, however, my concerns grew. In fact, I arranged for my associates with the German police to follow him on the occasion the *Heraldic* berthed in Hamburg. Sad to say, my intuition paid off. He went to the *Reeperbahn* to see an elderly German with a knowledge of firearms—blind as it so happens—who, curiously enough, arrived at the rendezvous with two canes—and left with only one."

"Von Herder!" I exclaimed.

At that moment, like a warning cry, the train sounded its horn. We must have been getting close to Horsham.

"Quite so, old fellow," replied Holmes, ignoring the blast from the horn, "Von Herder, the gun mechanic. It was he, I have come to believe, who furnished Jack Ferguson with an air rifle. Though not the most talented of gunsmiths, Von Herder is competent enough. Not only could he obtain from gun-makers like Townsend and Reilly the basics of the hollow walking stick, but he could also combine the structural framework with the mechanism of his own air gun. Jack would certainly not be the first shooter to employ a rifle that resembled a walking stick. But I hazard a guess that he may be the first to render the employment of *both* of its features a necessity."

"Of course!" I exclaimed. "A malformed assassin concealing his weapon in the guise of a dependable cane."

"Quite so, old fellow. It may have been no more than coincidence that the *Heraldic* was delivering a shipment of tea to New York in early January of this year, but I'm willing to wager that Jack was no longer part of the crew when it left a week later. He had honed his skills with the rifle and somehow presented himself as an accomplished shooter to the lawless elements bent on exploiting America's East Coast.

"Word travels fast within the criminal underworld, and Jack must have learned that his services could be put to use in Kentucky. It mattered little that the *Heraldic* had sailed before the deed was done. No doubt he earned plenty for his work and could easily book passage back to England. My hope in meeting with your friend Ferguson, Watson, is simply to confirm my reasoning."

*****

Though a closed carriage conveyed us the few miles from Horsham to Lamberley, we had to hire an open dogcart for the final leg of the journey. A thin rain began as soon as we reached the road to Cheeseman's, forcing us to wrap ourselves more tightly in our long coats and pull our hats even lower over our brows. Only when we recognised the familiar winding lane of Sussex clay did we know our ever-dampening excursion was about to end.

No doubt, it was the unkind weather that made the seventeenth-century farmhouse appear more ominous than I had remembered. To be sure, the leaden skies and shadowy trees had darkened its redbrick walls, but I was certain that some element beyond the weather was rendering the atmosphere so oppressive.

"I have to admit to you, Mr Holmes," said a sombre Bob Ferguson, who met us personally at the dark-oak outer door, "that I'm of mixed minds talking with you. There's no two ways about it." Without so much as the briefest of smiles, he continued to speak as he slowly ushered us inside. "I will never forget the joy you restored to my life by revealing the causes of my wife's strange behaviour. And yet, though I know it was for the best, I cannot forgive you for compelling me to remove my Jacky from our family."

The reluctant host led us into a dimly-lit sitting room where bright flames danced in a cavernous fireplace, casting eerie patterns on the half-oak, half-plastered walls. Ferguson offered us each a brandy and motioned to seats on the leather couch, but his tone was anything but warm.

Recounting the recent history of his son Jack was obviously not to Ferguson's liking. After Holmes had asked what Ferguson knew of Jack's latest activities, the father required a pull of the brandy and began his report with a frown. "When Jacky returned home following his first voyage—it's been about two years now—I was hoping to see a positive change in the lad's attitude. Unfortunately, there was anything but. Oh, he did ask if we might go out shooting, not a sport in which he had showed a whit of interest prior to his putting out to sea. But he shot some grouse, don't you know, and seemed quite pleased with himself. At the very least, I thought the outing might help us strengthen our friendship, but he remained here just a day or two. In point of fact, gentlemen, he collected his belongings and told us he would be taking a flat in London, thank you very much. Then he left, making off with my German dictionary for good measure. I haven't seen him since."

"Do you know his current location, Mr Ferguson?" Holmes asked. "We have every suspicion that he has returned to London, and it is necessary for me to speak with him."

Ferguson scowled. "Is he in trouble again?"

"One can't be certain," Holmes replied. "That is why I need to see him."

I assumed that the boy's actual address was unimportant to Holmes. Certainly, the Baker Street Irregulars had dogged Jack Ferguson closely enough to identify his residence. Still, had his father known the boy's whereabouts, it would have made finding Jack that much more simple.

"No," said Ferguson, his voice laced with bitterness, "he's never shared that detail with me. If he had, I'm not certain I would want to share it with you. The boy has been through enough."

Holmes nodded. Later he would explain to me, "I wanted to learn just how estranged father and son had become. That the father doesn't know where his son is living indicates the severity of their break."

During our visit, we saw no sign of either Mrs Ferguson or the young boy who had been the target of Jacky's wrath those few years before. But having exhausted our topic, we finished our brandies, thanked a sceptical Ferguson for his help, and promised to keep him up-to-date concerning any developments that involved his son. Then, with the much-appreciated aid of Ferguson's carriage, Holmes and I made our way back through the rain and wind to the small railway station in Horsham and ultimately home to Victoria and Baker Street.

Ringing in our ears throughout the journey, however, was Ferguson's final and unwarranted valediction: "None of this would have ever happened, Mr Holmes, had we not initially followed your cruel advice."

*****

I leave to my fair-minded readers the question of premeditation. For my part, I have never been totally clear concerning the exact role Holmes played in the shooting that concludes this account. At the very least, however, we have arrived at the point in the narrative that, as I have already indicated, presents Sherlock Holmes at his most cold-blooded.

Unfriendly winds had been blowing throughout the night of our return to Baker Street; and yet even as I was shuffling down the stairs for breakfast the following morning, I encountered my friend enveloped in cape and deerstalker entering our sitting room from the outer hall.

"Out so early in this foul weather?" I asked.

"Indeed," he answered, hanging his cold-weather garments on the pegs by the door. "Windy or not, it seemed the right time for the Trout boy to show me Jack's lodgings. Sooner than later, I wanted to ascertain the lie of the land. As it turns out, Jack maintains a flat in the Hanover Buildings in Tooley Street."

"Just south of the river—not far from the London Bridge Station?"

"Quite so," Holmes nodded.

"I know the place—five identical six-storey blocks of yellow brick." I had ministered to a few of its residents when I had worked as a houseman at Bart's. Originally constructed to house the men who laboured at the nearby docks and warehouses, the buildings had been renamed the Devon Mansions during the Great War. As far as I was concerned, Jack Ferguson could not have found a residence of lesser distinction.

"And yet," I was forced to concede, "the location makes sense. It's near London Bridge Station, and from there it's a simple train ride to Gravesend where Jack's ship put out." Though not overly familiar with the South Eastern and Chatham railway lines that ran parallel to the Thames, I still would not soon forget the foul-weather excursion through which Holmes and I had suffered on the line the previous year when we travelled to Gravesend to meet the so-called "Baron of Brede Place". I refer, of course, to the American writer Stephen Crane who was returning to England following his adventures in Cuba during the Spanish-American War.[*]

Equally memorable was a trip we had taken along that same course a few years before. To gain an early start at resolving the business with Professor Coram and the golden pince-nez at Yoxley Old Place, we had boarded a train at six in the morning at Charing Cross, the first station west of London Bridge. The plan had been to get off just beyond Chatham at the Higham halt, which is within a few miles of Yoxley.

As luck would have it, however, we found ourselves on the "slow" train, the one that stopped at every last station along the way. Inspector Hopkins had required only ninety minutes to cover the identical distance the day before, and yet it took us twice as long to make the same journey. That infernal train ride seemed to last forever! The thought still rankles.

Interrupting my memories, Holmes held up a small piece of paper. "I've taken the liberty to write Jack Ferguson a note in your name."

"In *my* name?" I replied. "Why not in *yours*? It is with you he has a quarrel, not with *me*. *You're* the one who suggested he go to sea."

"Precisely, my dear fellow. No love lost there, I'm afraid, which is quite the point. I don't think he'd agree to see *me*. A request from *you*, on the other hand, might make him curious enough to want to hear you out."

---

[*] Interested readers may find Watson's account of his and Holmes' encounter with Stephen and Cora Crane in Watson's narrative titled *Sherlock Holmes and the Baron of Brede Place*. (DDV)

"And just what did I say in this note?"

"You've asked permission to visit his flat."

"For what purpose?"

"Why, to request that he invite *me* in as well."

I thought my friend must be losing his senses. Had Holmes not just suggested that Jack would not welcome him? For that matter, Holmes suspected him of being a killer. Would it be safe for *me* in the lair of an assassin? Unable to mask my fears, I cast a concerned look at Holmes.

"Nothing to worry about, old fellow," said he. "I'll be standing just outside the building. Once he gives his approval, your job will be to open a window, and call me in."

I scratched my head in dismay. But knowing better than to question the rationality of my friend, I agreed to go along with his request. Still, as Holmes gave the page-boy the message for Jack Ferguson, I could not keep from wondering what trick my friend had up his sleeve.

Nothing to say to you, ran the note (including the underscoring) that Billy returned to me. *But I am curious about what you have to say to me. This afternoon. 2.00.* It was signed *JF*.

"Perfect," said Holmes, rubbing his hands together. "Now I have some last-minutes plans to put in motion. I'll be back at noon for lunch. Suggest beef sandwiches to Mrs Hudson. That joint I saw in the kitchen looked quite inviting."

And then he was gone.

*****

A hansom brought us to the Hanover Buildings just south of the Thames. The winds had died, but frantic traffic laden with tea and coffee and hops and leather bustled along

73

Tooley Street as the nearby ships and warehouses and shops made their demands.

No sooner did we exit the hansom than Holmes pointed to the block nearest us. "That's his room," he said, indicating the second window in the first-floor line. "He'll be expecting you. Go." With that, Holmes turned his back and began to survey the other structures along both sides of the street.

A gate interrupted the short black railing round the building, and I made my way through it as well as through the unlatched outer door. Traversing a dark foyer, I climbed the equally dark stairs to the first storey and in the light of a meagre gas lamp managed to locate what I presumed to be the second flat facing the street. I knocked hesitantly and, receiving no response, knocked again more sharply. This time the door swung open, and I immediately found myself standing face to face with Jack Ferguson.

When we first had met, Jacky had been able to conceal the hatred he harboured towards his infant half-brother. Only when Holmes confronted him regarding the boy's foul plan did Jacky's murderous intent reveal itself. Now, however, with his thick, flaxen hair combed straight back, that same devilish look appeared permanently etched into his features. His knotted brow, curling lip, and narrow, brutish eyes conveyed a rage that he clearly no longer felt compelled to hide. Worse, as much as one might hope to deny it, his deformity added to his sense of menace. For though I would be the first to protest the casting of so general an aspersion, in this instance his twisted spine seemed to reflect his twisted nature.

"I welcome you to my home," said he, bidding me enter with an exaggerated sweep of his arm. He indicated an old armchair, which I took; and pulling out one of two wooden chairs nesting under a rickety table, he sat down with his bent-back to the window. I recognised the trick, one often employed by Holmes himself. With the window behind him, Jack's face became silhouetted by the brightness outside, the result rendering his facial reactions difficult to discern.

"I don't see my father much," he offered. "I should imagine that you came at his request—though I don't know how you discovered this place."

I thought of Sammy Trout and the Irregulars; but playing my cards close to the vest, I said rather cryptically, "As you know, I work with Sherlock Holmes; and when he wants to find someone, that person is found."

"Holmes!" Jack spat out, "the man who tore me from my family? The man who turned me into what I have become?" The more animated he grew, the more spasmodically his entire body jerked.

"Holmes wishes to speak with you," said I calmly, "but he fears that you wouldn't let him through the door."

"He's got that right. Quite the detective!"

"Holmes anticipated you would react in such a fashion. That is why he asked me to pave the way. He was hoping I might talk you into letting him come up here. You see, he's just outside the building, awaiting a sign from me at the window to summon him in."

With some effort, Jack turned his body and glanced suspiciously at the window behind him. White curtains of gauze-linen barely covered the glass.

"What does he want with me?" Jack questioned.

"I'm sure I don't know. Why not let me signal that he can come up?"

Jack glanced at his bureau, a sure giveaway that something he wanted lay concealed within. Except for drumming his fingers on the table next to him, however, he sat motionless for a moment or two. At last, with a sigh of resignation, he said "Why not? "and waved me towards the window.

All I had left to do was carry out my instructions from Holmes. I spread the two curtains apart and then pulled up the sash. Holmes was pacing below, his eyes fixed on the window in search of any movement. I motioned for him to come up, at the same time being sure—as, for some strange reason, he had directed—to leave the window open and the curtains separated.

No sooner had I completed the task than I turned round and discovered myself face to face with the revolver Jack was now pointing at my head. As if playing a chord on a piano, he had arched the fingers of his free hand on the top of the bureau, their obvious strength helping him maintain his balance.

"No need for the gun," said I.

"Just a precaution." He pointed the barrel at the chair I had occupied. "Now sit."

I did, and with Jack still standing, we silently awaited the arrival of Sherlock Holmes.

Minutes later came a quick rap.

"Enter," commanded Jack, the barrel of the gun now turned toward the doorway.

Holmes walked in cautiously, eyed the pistol, displayed his empty hands, and opened wide his coat to show that he carried no weapons.

Motioning with the gun, Jack gestured for him to sit down.

Holmes pulled the second wooden chair away from the table, placed it to my right—opposite Jack—and turned it slightly so it wasn't in direct line with the window. He then seated himself and faced the gunman.

"Now, Mr Sherlock Holmes," said Jack, "be so kind as to inform me of the nature of your business."

Holmes flashed a brief smile and then, after stealing a glance at the window, got straight to the point. "I merely wish to ascertain, Jack Ferguson, that it was *not* the L & N Railroad that hired you to assassinate Governor Goebel in the American state of Kentucky last month."

For a man holding a gun, Jack displayed an alarming lack of control. His eyebrows shot up and he lurched backward upon hearing Holmes's charge. "Who claims that I assassinated anyone?" he demanded.

This time Holmes's smile lingered. "Please, Jack, don't take us for fools. We know of your recently acquired talent with guns. We know a man of your description was seen in the Capitol grounds in Frankfort. We know you met with the gun-maker von Herder in Hamburg when your ship put into port there last year, and thus we suspect that the walking stick you utilised in Frankfort was, in fact, an air rifle constructed by the German. Finally, we know that after shooting the governor, you boarded a railway in Kentucky, secured a ship in New York, and ended up here in Tooley Street."

Jack Ferguson's demeanour grew darker with each point ticked off by Holmes. "If you know so much, Mr Sherlock Holmes, how come you don't know who hired me?"

"That is why I am here, Jack, to find that out— before we hand you over to the authorities for shipment back to the United States."

"Ha!" he snorted. "That's funny with me holding the gun. Though I don't suppose it matters all that much since neither one of you is leaving here alive. When I explain to the police that I found two men burglarising my flat and shot them dead, you won't be in a position to tell them otherwise."

Shooting us dead? Consider me foolish; but though I had already experienced some concern for our safety, I had not anticipated so deadly a turn of events. Oh, I suspected that Holmes might enter the flat unarmed, and yet I also assumed that he would have some sort of plan for extricating us from this dilemma. Gazing at Jack's pistol caused me to see how naïve my thinking had been.

"I don't mind telling you," said Jack, "that L & N had nothing to do with the job in Frankfort. I was hired by a fellow called Rounceville—though I doubt that's his real name, and I don't really care because his money is good. He was a deputy to the Secretary of State in Kentucky, that fellow Powers; but I tell you honestly that I don't know if Powers even knew what was going on. This Rounceville told me the Republicans didn't want Goebel, a Democrat, stealing the election; and that to stop him once and for all, they wanted him dead. They told me when and where to lie in wait and promised diversionary gunfire when I performed the work. With my silent airgun, I knew I could shoot Goebel and escape undetected."

Holmes nodded. "As I thought," said he. Then he slowly stood and moved his chair to the right.

I suppose Jack could have shot him right then, but in point of fact he himself moved opposite Holmes placing his back squarely in front of the open window.

Holmes and I have been in some tight places together—but I cannot recall a moment that seemed more dire, a situation that seemed to offer no escape.

"Exit Sherlock Holmes," announced Jack, holding out his arm at full length as he pointed the pistol at my friend.

Suddenly—without a sound—a blossom of red erupted from Jack's white shirtfront. There was a momentary look of surprise that splashed across Jack's face, and then he fell forward. In a sense, it appeared that he had exploded from within; but the truth, of course, was much less fantastical. He had been struck by a bullet fired through the open window. That I had heard no report accompanying the shot made it all the more perplexing.

Needless to say, I sprang to my feet to administer to the stricken young man. I felt for a pulse, but there was none. Jack Ferguson lay dead; the man who had killed Governor Goebel had himself been assassinated.

Sherlock Holmes stood by the window staring silently across the street. Only then did it dawn on me that he had set up the entire deadly scheme.

"Holmes," I said, but he hushed me with a forefinger to his lips.

"Come," said he, and together we exited, leaving the body of Jack Ferguson sprawled on the floor of his flat in an ever-widening pool of blood. When we reached the pavement, Holmes hailed a hansom, and we made our return to Baker Street.

*****

"Not a word till dinner," said Sherlock Holmes in reference to our harrowing afternoon. "I have made plans with Mr Steele to meet us in Simpson's at 7.00. We shall discuss the matter then."

Leaving me to stand in wonder, Holmes retired to his bedroom; and soon I heard the strains of his violin as he attacked some concerto or other. For my part, I tried to pass the hours by reading the latest *Lancet* and keeping up-to-date on medical matters. But it did little good. I could not stop myself from wondering whether Holmes had possessed the notion of having Jack Ferguson shot from the start.

More practical queries coursed through my brain as well. The questions may appear obvious, but still I needed to learn who had actually done the shooting and why I had heard no shot fired? For that matter, I also wanted to know what had happened to the body Holmes and I had left on the floor of the flat and how my friend Robert Ferguson was to be told of the death of his son.

The answers to the first two questions came immediately upon my seeing Wyatt Steele at Simpson's. He entered the dining hall with the aid of a walking stick. Holmes and I were already sampling a pre-prandial sherry when the Pinkerton approached our table. As he settled into his seat, he carefully rested the stick against the chair's wooden arm. The significance of such a piece, especially in the hands of an accomplished agent like Steele, revealed all. The stick was a weapon fashioned by the gun-maker Von Herder.

"It is a little-known fact, Watson," said Holmes, "that the original air-rifle we'd taken from Sebastian Moran in '94 and bestowed upon Scotland Yard for safe-keeping had been misplaced and ultimately stolen. It seems that on his way to the Yard, Inspector Lestrade had alighted to quell some disturbance or other and left the thing in the hansom.*

---

* In his essay, "Colonel Moran's Infamous Air Rifle", (BSJ, Vol. 10, No 3, 1960), Ralph A. Ashton corroborates the theft of Moran's weapon. (DDV)

"One of my Irregulars happened to be near the vehicle at the time. Happily, he managed to grab the rifle and bring it to me. As the one who had presented it to Lestrade, in the first place, I concluded that the thing would be far safer in my hands than in his. Since then, I've kept it—along with the ammunition I bought—secure in one of my London hidey-holes. Today, however, when the business with Jack Ferguson materialised, I decided it might be needed to help extricate us from a delicate situation. Fortunately, Mr Steele, who was positioned on a rooftop across the road, was up to the task. He is, just as I had surmised, an American sharpshooter."

Steele's face flushed. "This gun is a fine piece, Mr Holmes. Make no mistake. You did your part by manoeuvring Ferguson to the window, but I never would have fired if he hadn't pointed his pistol at you."

"I believe I also speak for Dr Watson when I say that we are both extremely glad that you did."

I raised my glass in appreciation, and the three of us drank to Steele's timely marksmanship.

"In anticipation of the other questions I assume you have concocted," Holmes said to me, "you will be pleased to know that I have anonymously notified the police of the presence of a body in the Hanover Buildings. I leave it to the Yarders to inform Robert Ferguson of the death of his son. I don't believe he wants to hear anything more from you or me."

I felt a pang of guilt at not addressing Ferguson myself, but I have come to agree with Holmes's assessment of our intrusion into his life.

"I will also give to Mr Steele," Holmes continued, "a note in my own hand to pass along to his employers at the L & N Railroad. To protect Robert Ferguson's good name,

I've written that, whilst not offering the identity of the prime actor in the plot, the assassin exonerated L & N in the planning of Goebel's murder. I believe my reputation in the States is strong enough to alleviate any anxieties at the railroad. It is, of course, near impossible to put an end to the common gossip and speculation that will no doubt go on indefinitely."

"I'm much obliged to you for putting the record straight," said Steele. Holding up his glass once more, he added, "To Birdy Edwards. It was he, after all, who set me on the track to Baker Street and ultimately to the revelation of Goebel's true killer."

"Birdy Edwards," Holmes and I chorused, both of us in agreement that the late Pinkerton would have been duly pleased at the outcome of our investigation. No sooner had Holmes put down his glass than he signalled for the waiter to have one of the domed silver trollies brought to our table.

"One final question, Holmes," I asked before the carver arrived. "Do you not feel responsible for leading Jack Ferguson to his death?"

My friend stared into my eyes. "The man had become a hired killer, Watson, a paid assassin. However much I am to blame for his departure from this world, the regret does not give me much pause."

With that, we all turned our attention towards the trolley that was just then arriving before us.

*****

Following Holmes's retirement in 1903 to a cottage in Sussex, he and I saw each other only sparingly. Yet long after our involvement in the death of Jack Ferguson, we continued to keep track of the latest legal developments regarding the assassination of William Goebel.

Thanks to the accounts of pressmen like Irvin Cobb and our friend David Graham Phillips (himself the victim of an assassin's bullet in 1911), we could follow the evolution of the legal entanglements related to primary figures in the case. It was on 21 May 1900, just a few months after Goebel's death, that the United States Supreme Court ruled on the legitimacy of Goebel's gubernatorial victory over Republican William Taylor. Citing the argument of states' rights, the Court refused to overturn Goebel's election that had earlier been upheld by the Democratically-inclined Supreme Court of Kentucky.

On the other hand, appeals courts dominated by Republicans nullified the convictions of Caleb Powers and James Howard. Although Powers himself would face three more trials and actually be convicted in two of them, sympathetic courts demanded new trials both times, the last concluding with what the Americans term a "hung jury"— that is, the members of the jury were not in agreement, and the case was dismissed.

Like Powers, Howard, the presumed gunman, also faced another trial; but though unlike his associate he was convicted, in 1908 both he and Powers were finally pardoned. For his part, Youtsey, the alleged go-between, was paroled in 1916 and pardoned three years later. In the end, Caleb Powers, who had been tried four times for murder without success, was elected to the United States Congress in 1911. He would go on to serve four successive terms.

One evening some years after the various aspects of the Goebel affair had been settled, Holmes came up to London. Whilst enjoying cigars together in my sitting room, we found ourselves discussing the contradictory resolution of the entire business.

"If I recall correctly, Watson," Holmes observed, "in the case you titled 'The Abbey Grange', you recorded an observation of mine regarding the law. At the time, I said that I would rather play tricks with the law of England than with my own conscience. Is that not right?"

"Yes, Holmes," I said with a nod, "I believe you quote yourself correctly."

"Well then, " said he stretching out his long legs and exhaling a plume of blue smoke, "allow me to also say that, judging from all we have learned in the Goebel case, it would appear that in America it is the law that plays the tricks and one's conscience that suffers."

I nodded; and both of us, yet again contemplating the protean relationship between England and the United States, proceeded to fill the room with ever-thickening clouds of smoke.

An Adventure in Darkness

"You don't understand," he cried in a voice
that was meant to be great and resolute, and which broke. "You
are blind, and I can see . . . ."
                                        --H.G. Wells
                                        "The Country of the Blind"

*D*uring the twenty years I had known Sherlock Holmes, I had come to accept his various eccentricities. The chemical experiments on the scarred wooden table, the bullet holes in our wall, the letters transfixed with a blade to the mantel—all these I had learned to tolerate. But seeing Holmes that November afternoon in '01—eyes hidden behind a black silk cloth, Alpine walking stick in hand, and posed at the centre of our dismantled sitting room motionless as a statue—I thought that perhaps the poor man had finally lost his senses.

It was late in the day, and I had just completed an invigorating round of billiards at the club with my old friend Thurston. The autumnal winds were blowing; and as I walked along the Strand, contemplating a sweet sherry and warm fire, the thought of Holmes's strange activities never crossed my mind. No sooner did I enter our Baker Street lodgings, however, than I realised my simple plans for the remainder of the afternoon had come off the rails.

The sitting room lay in shambles. In spite of the golden streaks of sun still lighting the sky, the green damask curtains were already closed. And yet even in the darkness, I could see that the place looked as if Lear's hurricanoes had passed through. The two armchairs had been shoved aside; a stool, knocked over. Under a scattering of newspapers, the bearskin rug lay in a heap. Shards of a broken yellow saucer decorated the floor, an overturned yellow cup leaving black coffee stains on the white tablecloth.

In the midst of all this mayhem, the blindfolded Holmes, clad in his mouse-coloured dressing gown, cocked an ear. "Watson," said he, "is that you?"

"Of course, it is I. Who else should it be? What on earth has possessed you?"

Holmes pulled up one side of the blindfold and, Cyclops-like, peered at me with a single grey eye. "I am soon to be visited by a blind young lady, and I was endeavouring to understand what having no sight must be like."

"But, Holmes," I protested, "you know every inch of this room. The placement of the chairs is part of your interviewing strategy, and you regularly count the number of steps from the outer door. If you pardon the redundancy, you could navigate this room blindfolded."

"Right you are, old fellow—which is why I asked Mrs Hudson to draw the curtains and to move things randomly about whilst my eyes remained covered. She was none too pleased with the task, I can assure you."

With a shake of my head, I turned up the gas to bring light to the room.

"*Fiat lux*," Holmes said, tossing the blindfold towards a chair. "I am afraid I did bump the table. Hence, the broken plate and the overturned cup."

I shook my head at Holmes's behaviour. "Who is the woman that has prompted all this?" I asked whilst righting the fallen stool. "A case, I presume?"

"Quite so," said he as he stooped to recover the newspapers from the rug. "She is called Anna Nuñez. You may have read in the *Times* of her husband, Juan Carlos Nuñez, the famed mountaineer from Colombia. He has just come back to England after having been lost for months whilst off trekking somewhere in the Andes. They have been married for only a short while."

"I cannot say that I remember the story; but if he is no longer missing, then what can his wife wish to speak to you about?"

"That, my friend," smiled Holmes, "I am afraid I cannot deduce." He was now employing his stick to flatten the lingering waves in the rug. "The request came via an oral message from her servant earlier today. Other than forewarning me that his mistress lacked sight, he had no knowledge of the matter in question." Holmes consulted the clock on the mantel. "She is due here at 5.00."

"Why, that is in less than a quarter hour!" I cried. "We must put the rest of these things back more quickly."

"Your enthusiasm suggests you wish to join the consultation."

"Of course I do," said I, "if I am invited."

"It goes without saying, old fellow," answered Holmes who, not without some amusement, was watching me attempt to set the armchairs at just their proper angles.

Holmes proceeded to prop his stick against the wall nearest the door; and I, taking care to wrap the coffee cup and pieces of broken plate within the stained tablecloth, moved the whole mess out of sight. Only after a final glance round the room assured me that we had corrected all of Mrs Hudson's handiwork did I feel comfortable in announcing, "All is in order."

"Well and good," said Holmes with single clap of his hands, "—though I am certain Mrs Nuñez will not notice the difference."

"Holmes," said I, ignoring the callousness of his remark, "we cannot have the poor woman tripping over the *débris* of your little experiment."

With another check of the clock, Holmes exchanged his dressing gown for a jacket. Fortunately, I had remained in my coat, for we did not have much longer to wait. Indeed, it was just a matter of minutes before we heard Mrs Hudson helping someone climb the stairs.

"Here we are, my dear," said our landlady just beyond the door, and then there was a sharp rap. "Mr Holmes," she called with motherly concern, "let's not keep this young lady waiting, shall we."

Holmes swung wide the door, and Mrs Hudson, casting an approving eye round the neatened sitting room, guided an attractive young woman into our presence.

"Mrs *Nunez*," our landlady announced, omitting the nasalisation called for by the tilde. Despite her polite attentiveness, Mrs Hudson's mispronunciation of the Spanish name exhibited the same acerbic tone she employed when referring to all manner of foreigners. Indeed, having delivered to Sherlock Holmes his client, our landlady seemed eager to depart the scene and quickly closed the door as she exited.

"Mr Sherlock Holmes?" the woman enquired in impeccable English.

I am bound to admit that with a surname of Nuñez, I had expected a dark-skinned, dark-haired lady. But now I realised that the appellation belonged to her husband and that the blonde young woman standing before us was properly English. With skin as white as porcelain and a dress of burgundy velvet, she looked like someone ready to step out for an evening's entertainment. Her hair was done up in a fashionable *chignon;* her small features were pleasing to observe. And yet, of course, she was blind.

No smoke-lensed spectacles concealed her affliction; and yet one could not detect whether the orbs appeared rheumy or glazed because in point of fact her eyes were simply closed. Detracting not a whit from her beauty, her eyelids, rimmed as they were with long, dark lashes, appeared capable of opening at any moment. It was as if she were Sleeping Beauty awaiting the kiss of a handsome prince.

"Mr Holmes?" she asked again, at the same time, pivoting her head slowly to the left and right.

"I am Sherlock Holmes, Madam," said he.

Upon hearing his voice, Mrs Nuñez turned to face him. "I am Anna Nuñez," she said, extending an ungloved hand. "Please forgive the informality, but because I rely so much on my sense of touch, I find gloves to be an encumbrance."

"Understood, Madam," said Holmes as his long fingers enveloped hers.

The lady turned her head in *my* direction. "Is there someone else present?"

"Indeed there is," Holmes said. "Standing next to me is my friend and associate, Dr John Watson. I assure you that you may speak as freely to him as you do to me."

"Charmed," said I. "Allow me to offer you a seat." And I took the liberty of placing a deferential hand on her arm as I guided her to a chair.

"It is unusual to have someone with your condition visit us, Mrs Nuñez," said Holmes as we seated ourselves opposite her. "Other than the fact that you have been blind from birth, that you do not like coffee, and that you are an accomplished pianist, I really cannot imagine what more I can tell you."

Mrs Nuñez's eyebrows shot up in amazement. "I—I have heard of your powers, Mr Holmes, but I must confess that you take my breath away. How do you know such details about me?"

"Elementary, Mrs Nuñez. You set your head so instinctually to listen for vital sounds and to catch stray aromas that one must assume you have cultivated the employment of compensatory senses since birth. You frowned when you detected the lingering aroma of our spilt coffee—hence, my inference that you do not like the brew. And then there are the calluses on the pads of your fingers— I felt them when we shook hands—thus, my reference to someone who frequents the piano keyboard."

"I might have been a typist," she shot back. "Memorisation of the placement of the machine's keys allows the blind to type, you know."

Holmes's quick smile indicated his appreciation of the woman's perceptiveness.

"I am afraid," said he, "that the rough spots at the outside edges of your thumbs are the quite distinctive results of striking keys in distant octaves. Such stretching is more common to the pianist than to anything a typist is required to perform."

"I fear," said she with a demure little chuckle, "that I shall have to wear gloves in the future."

"A trifle, Madam, I assure you. Yet I repeat that I am at a loss to suggest why you have come to see me."

Mrs Nuñez adjusted the small black reticule she held in her lap. "Let me first apologise for calling on you at so late an afternoon hour. But I must tell you that time is measured quite differently by those who cannot see."

"Is it not true," I offered, "that, when contemplating sleep, the blind relate more to heat and cold than to light and darkness?"

"Indeed, Doctor. I for one often find myself at odds with the schedules of sighted people. I am, you see, a very late riser and, as a result, tend to remain awake till the late hours of the night."

"The sleep patterns of the blind," murmured Holmes. "I confess it is a topic to which I have not given much thought. Perhaps I shall write a monograph on the subject. I would expect that your husband might be able to contribute some relevant observations regarding your own behaviour."

Holmes's mention of the woman's husband caused a reaction. She tightened her grip on her reticule and knit her brow. "It is about my husband that I wish to speak, Mr Holmes, though I imagine you came to the same conclusion, and that is why you so deftly brought the conversation back to Juan Carlos."

Holmes smiled again, another sign of respect for the woman's acumen though, of course, she herself could not see these responses. Holmes must have wondered, as did I, if Mrs Nuñez understood that in relation to a female client, trouble with a husband was always a safe guess for any detective to venture.

"For you gentlemen to understand our marriage," she continued, "I think that an explanation of my background would be helpful. I am sure you have realised that my trappings of success do not typify the conditions experienced by most sightless people. For them, life has not been so accommodating."

"By all means," I said, "tell us your story."

"My mother was an actress of no great repute," Mrs Nuñez explained. "And my father left her once he discovered that their baby could not see. But my mother was a fighter and would not allow her daughter to be pitied or condemned or even ridiculed—the way too many with my condition are treated in our society. She worked hard and saved enough money to enrol me in the Royal Normal College for the Blind here in London."

"That would be the school in Upper Norwood," I observed. I myself had directed a blind patient to that institution. It was renowned for its worthwhile programs.

"The very same. My mother heard that the school had been designed for children like me. That turned out to be true. In addition to my regular studies, I learned to read Braille and to play the piano. The college is well known for the piano tuners it has produced, but such work is generally reserved for men. None the less, I sharpened my craft; and when I was not mastering how to tune the instrument, I was perfecting my ability to play it. I grew quite skilled in the art; and whilst I would never think of performing at the Royal Albert Hall, I have been invited to play at various smaller venues here in London."

"Would that we had a piano," I said without thinking. Obviously, the woman was a client seeking help from a detective, not a pianist in need of an audience.

"It was at my performance of Chopin's *Études* in late March," she continued, "that I was approached by Juan Carlos Nuñez, he who was destined to become my husband. I could tell from touching his face—he has a straight nose and a square chin—that he was a handsome man. And I soon learned how, thanks to his mountaineering skills, he had made not only a name for himself among the rich but also the money to go along with it.

"Juan Carlos could have had his pick of many sighted women, and yet for some reason he seemed obsessed with me. Perhaps I should have recognised the danger signs then. But he followed me to my various concerts, took me to dinner, courted me, and in late May— within two months of our having met—asked to marry me."

"Only two months," I observed judgementally. "Not a lengthy courtship."

"No, indeed, Doctor. I was, in fact, a June bride." She added this last bit with the blush of a little girl. Within a moment, however, her mood grew sombre again. "You forget my condition, Doctor Watson. Any offer of marriage is far beyond what a blind woman can hope to expect—and I assure you that an offer from an attractive suitor like Juan Carlos Nuñez is not easily ignored. "

I knew that her charge was true. So compelling an image did this young woman present that one might almost be excused for forgetting her plight. Ignore the handkerchief she had removed from her reticule and begun to twist, and one might wrongly assume she had not a care in the world.

"In short, gentlemen, I accepted his proposal. We have been married for almost six months now, and it is only during the last few weeks that his behaviour has begun to disturb me."

Leaning back in his chair, Holmes steepled his fingers, as he was wont to do in anticipation of hearing the details of a case. "If you would, Madam," said he, "describe for us your concerns."

"Yes," said Mrs Nuñez with a sigh. "It is, after all, what I have come here for. My concerns go back about a month. It was then that Juan Carlos began muttering to himself."

"Muttering, you say?" asked Holmes. "Muttering what?"

"He repeats the same phrase over and over again—like a refrain. It is as if he is trying to reassure or convince himself of some strange matter. And he continues to this day."

Holmes bent forward, his grey eyes flashing. "And what is it that he says?"

"In the country of the blind," she said simply. "At least, that is all I can hear."

"'In the country of the blind'?" Holmes repeated.

"Nothing more?" I asked.

"Should there be more, Doctor? Needless to say, I am not well read. Does this phrase have some greater meaning?"

"It could be part of the old proverb," I responded, thinking of the common-enough utterance made by those with limited attributes who hoped to set themselves above those with even fewer. "In the country of the blind," I announced, "the one-eyed man is king."

Holmes did me one better; he stated it in Latin: "*In regione caecorum rex est luscus*—so stated the philosopher, Erasmus, in the early sixteenth century. Some trace the adage back to early Biblical interpretations."

A furrow marked the woman's brow. "I shall take your word for it, gentlemen, but what does it have to do with me? Juan Carlos and I live in Berkeley Square, not in some 'country of the blind'. And my husband certainly has the use of *both* of his eyes—not to mention his outstanding physical skill. He is most assuredly not someone of—what was your phrase, Doctor? —'limited attributes'."

"Sorry," I replied. "I had no intention—"

But Mrs Nuñez ignored my interruption. "I am at wit's end. When I ask him what he is saying, he just ignores me. Gentlemen, I do not understand why he should go about babbling some nonsense about a one-eyed man. Do you?"

Holmes did not answer immediately. Instead, he cast his gaze directly at our guest as he ruminated on her situation. It was a rude and intrusive posture, which he might have modified had she been able to observe him. At last, he said, "There is something else that troubles you, madam. I suspect that you have not told us all."

Mrs Nuñez lowered her head. With great difficulty, she admitted, "He—he has struck me, Mr Holmes."

"The blackguard!" I exploded. Hitting a woman is bad enough. But striking a blind person—woman or man—goes well beyond the pale.

"It was really more of a slap," she said. "But he had never done it before, and it goes without saying that I am easy prey. He apologised the first time he—"

"The *first* time!" I cried. "Do you mean to say there were more?"

She nodded. "That is why I came to see Mr Holmes, Doctor. I am afraid for my safety."

"Certainly the police—"

"Believe me, Doctor Watson," she said firmly, "I can assure you that the police take little interest in protecting wives from their husbands. There's many the judge who winks at wife-beating. And as for protecting the blind—let us just say that the odds against *us* are even worse."

I listened to her words, and I knew she spoke the truth.

Mrs Nuñez now turned back to my friend. "Mr Holmes, I was hoping that you could get to the bottom of what is causing Juan Carlos to behave as he does. For my own peace of mind, I have to believe his problem can be solved."

Sherlock Holmes does not easily display sympathy, but the knotting of his bushy brows told me that, like myself, he was greatly concerned for the welfare of this noble woman.

"I will help you, Madam," he said quickly.

She reached into her reticule once more and withdrew a small set of visitor's cards. They were held together with a red ribbon, and I would later learn that they contained her address in addition to her name. Slipping out the topmost, she offered it in Holmes's direction.

"Rest assured, Madam," said he as he snatched the card from her wavering hand, "we shall get to the bottom of this business." He moved his chair as he stood, a signal that we were finished, and Mrs Nuñez rose as well. "Watson will help you secure a cab," said Holmes and with a gesture of his head indicated my assignment.

It was a task I carried out with the utmost responsibility and concern. In fact, I carefully guided Mrs Nuñez to the stairwell, accompanied her down the stairs, and escorted her out to the kerb where I hailed a hansom. Only after she handed me another one of her cards to be given to the driver did I help her climb in.

*****

By the time I returned to our rooms, Sherlock Holmes had already begun reviewing the entries in his abstracts under the letter "N".

"Juan Carlos Nuñez, mountaineer," he announced as I sat down across the table from him. "Born in 1870 near Bogotá, Colombia. Mastered English at an early age, a diligent reader, sailed the seven seas, employed as a guide by numerous British hikers, including some of the most famous of the English aristocracy. Granted membership in the Alpine Club three years ago."

"Quite an accomplished fellow," I observed, "at least, in that line of work."

Even as I spoke, Holmes was reading ahead. "Listen to this, Watson," said he, raising a forefinger. "Apparently, Nuñez was thought to have died on his last excursion, this one near Quito, Ecuador. In May of last year, he replaced a Swiss guide, one of three leading a small group of Englishmen up Parascotopetl, the so-called "Matterhorn of the Andes". It was then that he disappeared. According to Pointer, a fellow-climber whose narrative is supposedly the best of the many written about Nuñez's disappearance,[*] they followed his tracks to the top of a long, steep slope. The disrupted snow revealed where he had lost his footing and tumbled to the bottom. Although there was no sign of the mountaineer himself, Pointer reported that they could just barely make out far below the edge of a sharp precipice over which, they presumed, Nuñez had fallen to his death. In light of the tragedy, the group discontinued the climb."

"But as we know from Mrs Nuñez," I pointed out, "that is not the end of the story."

"Correct," Holmes said without looking up from the text. "It says here that with little explanation, Nuñez

---

[*] Pointer, Nigel. *"The Disappearance of Juan Carlos Nuñez."* *Alpine Journal.* 1900 [annual]. (JHW)

reappeared in February of this year, about a month after the death of Queen Victoria."

"And it was just a month later," I added, "in March, that he met his soon-to-be wife."

"Quite so, Watson," said Holmes, closing the volume. "And yet in spite of Pointer's details, the stark truth remains that we have no information about what transpired between the time of Nuñez's disappearance and his return to civilization. It is a time-period for which we must account. To shield Mrs Nuñez from her husband's suspicions, we should begin our investigation at the Alpine Club. It is the London centre for all matters mountaineering, and you will recall that Nuñez is a member. We shall go there in the morning."

Having determined our plans for the following day, Holmes picked up his violin. A Bach partita was his choice on this particular evening. With all due respect to my friend, I would have preferred listening to Mrs Nuñez play Chopin on the piano.

*****

A breakfast of kippers, toast, and coffee preceded our departure for the Alpine Club the next morning. At 23, Savile Row, the club was situated not far from the Nuñez's house in Berkeley Square; and it was probably this very proximity that had caused Nuñez to establish his home there. Just as we were proceeding out the door, Holmes reached for his deerstalker and Inverness cape. The cold weather easily justified warm outerwear, but I believe that Holmes felt his *accoutrements* added credibility to his appearance as a hiker. I settled for my heavy coat.

The Alpine Club is located at the far end of Savile Row* next to the arched passageway to Conduit Street. The building includes a large meeting hall, a reading room, a map room and a library. In the lobby behind a desk of polished red-mahogany sat a bespectacled clerk, one Mr Horace Stringfellow according to the plaque in front of him, a slightly-built chap with middle-parted, black hair. Ironically, he appeared to offer no hint of a talent for mountain climbing.

Holmes presented himself to Stringfellow as a seasoned hiker looking for greater challenges. "I'm told," said Holmes, "that you have a guide here who's most adept at leading groups on foreign climbs. I've been up to the Reichenbach Falls and am currently thinking about an expedition to the Andes."

"The Andes?" Stringfellow queried.

"Yes, and I've heard that you have a member named Nuñez who's quite familiar with the area."

"Ah, yes, Nuñez," said Stringfellow. He absent-mindedly began spinning the small globe to the right of his desk blotter. "Actually, Nuñez had some problems on his last climb and, as yet, has not seemed interested in going out again." Stringfellow smiled. "Funny thing, though. You are the second person today asking about the man."

Holmes smiled at the emergence of an unexpected development. "Interesting," said he. "Was it someone else asking about a venture to South America?"

"No," replied the secretary, stopping the globe. "A writer, actually. But you can speak to him yourself. He said he would be stopping in the reading room. I have not seen

---

* The building was demolished in 1936 to allow the construction of a throughway to Conduit Street. (DDV)

him leave, so I presume he must still be there. It is just down the hallway to your left."

Holmes thanked the clerk, and we were already in the hall by the time Stringfellow's last sentence reached our ears: "We do have other guides to recommend, you know."

The reading room looked quite inviting. Rather than the bookshelves one would expect to find in such a room, however, the walls below an upper border of pale rosettes were bedecked with paintings, majestic renderings of the world's great mountains. Oh, I could appreciate their beauty readily enough, but not their individuality. To me one snow-capped mountaintop set against a bright blue sky looked much like another. Fortunately, each frame contained a title. Here was the Matterhorn; there, Mont Blanc. Here a portrait of the American Mt. Whitney; there, a picture of the African Kilimanjaro. Featuring explosions of red and yellow, one singularly dramatic piece depicted the imagined eruption of ancient Mt. Vesuvius.

Actual flames danced in the fireplace on the side wall; in the centre of the room stood an oval oak table laden with books, most all of them dealing with various climbing expeditions. Half a dozen chairs filled the room including two plush armchairs on either side of the fireplace. In the armchair facing the open door sat a familiar-looking gentleman with a narrow face, thick moustache, dark hair, and piercing eyes. He was reading a newspaper though looking up at the doorway every now and again.

"There is our writer," I whispered to Holmes in the hallway.

"I am impressed, Watson," he replied softly. "Besides the ink smudges on his fingers and the frayed edges of his cuffs, how can you be so certain?"

"Because I know the man, Holmes," said I confidently (in spite of missing the details Holmes had pointed out). "He is the fantasy writer, H.G. Wells. Author of such books as *The Time Machine* and *The War of the Worlds*."

Holmes nodded in recognition. "Too superficial for my taste, I am afraid."

"Not my style either," said I, "but still a pleasure to read. You will recall that I met him at Brede Place when I was visiting Stephen and Cora Crane. We struck up quite the friendship."*

Holmes and I entered the room, and immediately H.G. Wells studied my face. "Could that actually be Dr John Watson?" he asked in his high-pitched voice.

"It is indeed, Mr Wells," said I.

"Bertie," he reminded me.

"It is so good to see you again, Bertie. And may I present to you my friend, Mr Sherlock Holmes."

"Sherlock Holmes, at last," said Wells rising to his feet. "I missed you at that year's-end *fête* at Brede Place, you know."

The two men shook hands, each one seemingly taking the measure of the other—on the one side, a master of unravelling crimes; on the other, a master of spinning fantasies.

Wells invited us to sit, and Holmes took the unoccupied armchair whilst I pulled over the straight-backed chair from the book table and placed it between them.

---

* Interested readers may find Watson's account of his initial meeting with H.G. Wells in Watson's narrative titled *Sherlock Holmes and the Baron of Brede Place*. (DDV)

Holmes wasted no time with amenities. "Mr Wells, I must ask what brings you to the Alpine Club?"

"Just up from Spade House, our new home in Folkestone. I am always on the hunt for fresh story-material, you see; and I had heard some rumours from my hiking friends concerning a guide called Nuñez who had reportedly gone missing on an expedition to the Andes. Just my sort of thing. He was said to be connected to the Alpine Club here in London, so I came up to find out more about him."

"And did you?" Holmes wanted to know.

"That I did," chortled Wells. "In all due modesty, it was thanks to my literary reputation that the chap at the desk, Stringfellow, put me in touch with the man. Nuñez and I first met two days ago in this very room; and after I had agreed to give him an advance on half of any profits I might earn from writing about his travels, he agreed to bring me the notes he had made after having gone missing in the mountains. Believe me when I say that he hinted at having had quite an adventure in uncharted territory."

Holmes leaned forward. "And what, may I ask, did you learn, Mr Wells?"

The writer frowned. "With all due respect, Holmes, I am not one to give away the plots of my stories."

Sherlock Holmes narrowed his eyes. "I assure you, Mr Wells, that a person's life may hang in the balance."

"I should imagine no less," Wells said. "Else, why would Sherlock Holmes be involved? And yet even so . . . ."

My friend refused to be put off. "It is a young woman's life we are discussing here," said he. "But perhaps we can strike a bargain. Assuming that what we discover is not of a criminal nature and that, as a consequence, we do not have to involve the police, if you reveal to me what you have learned, I will do my utmost to see that you will be first to get any titbits we turn up in our investigation."

"I suppose that whether I agree or not depends on just what sort of investigation you are conducting."

Holmes took a deep breath. "Mr Wells," said he, "a moment ago you spoke of your own reputation. I ask you to consider the value of mine. I tell you again that a woman's life is at stake."

H.G. Wells stared at Sherlock Holmes for what seemed like a full minute. At last, with only the crackle of the fire breaking the silence, he nodded his assent; and I joined Holmes in leaning forward to hear Wells's account.

"This chap Nuñez told me of the horrific fall he suffered on his last climb in Ecuador. He tumbled from atop a towering precipice, and it was the soft snow upon which he landed that saved his life. Not only did he find himself in an unknown valley, but it was there that he also discovered a community of primitive villagers. They lived in stone huts totally isolated from the outside world. What is more, to his great frustration, surrounded as he was by towering mountains, massive glaciers, and dense forest, he could find no way out. After much futile searching, he concluded that he was going to have to live with these strange people."

"What made them so strange?" Holmes asked.

"Oh," said Wells, "did I not say? They were all blind. Been so for generations."

At the word "blind", Holmes and I exchanged glances. No doubt Holmes, like me, was recalling the proverb reported by Mrs Nuñez.

"Let me guess," I suggested to Wells. "When he discovered he could not find a way out, he quoted the old saying, 'In the country of the blind, the one-eyed man is king.'"

"Why, that is absolutely correct, Watson," cried Wells, clearly astonished by my prescience. "Nuñez figured that with all his knowledge, if he could not escape from these people, then at the very least he could become their leader. He would impress them with his grand knowledge of a world they knew nothing of—light, dark, colour, stars."

Sherlock Holmes shook his head. "To persons who have no frame of reference," he observed, "such concepts are most difficult to convey."

"Quite right, Holmes," Wells said. "The way Nuñez reported it, the people thought him mad. I should point out that all this did not occur overnight. Nuñez claims he has written an account that fills in the details, including his *affaire de cœur* with a young blind woman there. It seems his resolution to remain in the valley was enhanced by his infatuation with her."

"And yet," said I, "he attempted a dangerous and near-impossible escape in order to return to England."

Wells patted his moustache. "In the end, you see, he did find a way to climb out—a challenge he had considered hopeless till he finally worked up the courage to give it a go."

"But he could have been killed in the process," said I. "What made him take the risk?"

"Oh," said Wells again, "did I not say? To cure him of his so-called madness, the village leaders had decided to remove what they determined to be the cause of his derangement."

"And what was that?" the doctor in me wanted to know.

"Sorry. I seem to be omitting all the crucial bits. Perhaps I am just reluctant to reveal the best parts of the story I intend to write." Here Wells smiled and paused to stare into the fire. Like Sherlock Holmes, Wells too recognised the drama inherent in the facts behind a compelling narrative. Only after he reckoned enough time had passed to increase the suspense to its maximum did he resume. "It seems that the villagers had resolved to cure Nuñez of his madness by removing those two queer, distended growths that they felt just below his brow. After all, the villagers had no such appendages, and so they assumed those irritant bodies to be responsible for his problems. In short, gentlemen, they fully intended to put out his eyes."

The simple statement came like a thunderbolt. I no longer heard the outside din of voices, cries of hawkers, rattle of carriages. My own eyes would not focus. The conclusion of Wells's report seemed not unlike a death sentence for Juan Carlos Nuñez.

Now Holmes and I turned to stare into the fire. For his part, H.G. Wells, who apparently knew nothing of Nuñez's new wife, merely sat back in silence. We all remained that way for a few minutes.

It was Holmes who returned to the subject. "Mr Wells," said he, "you are a student of human psychology. What do you make of the fact that, upon his return, this Nuñez married a blind woman?"

"A blind woman, you say?" said Wells. "He never got round to telling me the most recent events in the story. But if one thinks about it, one should not be too surprised at such a marriage—at least, not if one remembers his Swift. Do you recall Gulliver's final voyage, his journey to the land of the Houyhnhnms?"

"The talking horses?" I recalled.

"The talking horses who were also philosophers," Wells reminded us. "Recall that when Gulliver returned to England, his distaste for human beings had grown so intense that he spent all his days in the barn with regular horses, the non-speaking kind. As I recollect, he said that 'the first Money' he laid out upon his return was to buy a pair of 'Stone-Horses',* and he admitted to conversing with them four hours each day."

Holmes flashed a smile. "You are suggesting that Nuñez was like Gulliver—that he may still have been so much in love with the blind lady he had left behind that he attempted to recreate the experience with a contemporary replacement. You are the literary man, sir; and yet I believe there are also readers who interpret Gulliver's admission as proof of his madness. I know that *I* do."

"Perhaps, you are right, Holmes. But why not see for yourself. Did I not say? The reason I have planted myself here is to meet with Mr Nuñez. In truth, he and I have an appointment at noon today."

Somewhere in the building a clock was striking that very hour. If the author of *The Time Machine* was correct, we should not have long to wait.

*****

After some five minutes had passed, H.G. Wells flicked his head at the open door. Holmes turned in that direction, and I looked to my right. Standing in the portal was a tall, dark-skinned man with a full, rich head of jet-black hair. Dressed in a snug brown suit, he was holding a

---

* Today we would call them stallions. (DDV)

bowler and gave a nod of recognition to Wells. Upon surveying Holmes and me, however, his expression changed. His brows knotted; and as he approached, the strong set of his jaw seemed to become all the more rigid.

"What's this then, Mr Wells?" the man asked with the faintest lilt of a Spanish accent. "You said nothing about bringing others to our meeting."

We all rose; and Wells attempted to introduce us, but Holmes was in no mood for delay.

"See here, Mr Nuñez," said he, "my name is Sherlock Holmes, and I believe you pose a threat to your wife. My associate Dr Watson and I have come to demand an explanation."

"I've heard of you, Mr Holmes," said Nuñez with a wry smile. "Many's the English mountaineer who carries your stories about in his rucksack. But that doesn't mean I'll tolerate your interference in my personal affairs." He turned to Wells and held out his palm. "You promised me money."

"You promised me your notes," Wells replied.

Nuñez patted his left breast as if to imply that his papers were stored in an inner pocket. "Now give me what's due," he insisted, still holding out his hand, "so I don't have to spend any more time with these pests."

Slowly, Wells withdrew a wallet from inside his coat and produced a number of notes.

Suddenly, Holmes grabbed Nuñez's extended wrist. "Tell me about your wife *now*!" he demanded, the abrupt action an obvious tribute to how much Holmes was worrying about his innocent client.

A beatific calmness suddenly seemed to engulf the mountaineer. *"¿Porqué no?"* he shrugged. "It matters little to me any longer."

Holmes let go his hold. "What do you mean?"

"Anna was a diversion," Nuñez said blandly, "a poor substitute for my true love, Medina-saroté. I am planning to return unencumbered to the country of the blind—and make her my bride."

"'Unencumbered', you say," repeated Holmes. "You plan to win some sort of divorce before you go." It was more a statement than a question.

"No, Mr Holmes, I intend to leave right now—from here in fact—as soon as I take my money."

Holmes nodded. "Then you will content yourself with becoming a bigamist?"

The word caused Nuñez to blanch. "No, I will *not!*" he proclaimed.

"What do you mean?" Holmes fairly shouted the question this time. "What have you *done*?"

Suddenly, Nuñez burst into maniacal laughter. It began as a high-pitched howl and devolved into a series of staccato barks. To this very day, the recollection of those animal sounds makes the hair on the back of my neck stand up.

Then just as suddenly, he turned complacent again. *"¿Quién sabe?"* he shrugged, gazing at Holmes.

My friend and the mountaineer locked eyes. In the moments that followed, it seemed that Holmes was picking the man's very brain.

Mere spectators, Wells and I watched as the two stared at each other. It was Nuñez who broke the tension with the wave of his hand. "Gentlemen," he exclaimed to all of us, *"adiós!"* And in an explosion of movement, he grabbed the banknotes, which still lay in Wells's hand, and raced out of the room. He paused only long enough to shout with a laugh, "She's a light sleeper, Holmes—be careful not to wake her!" and then he was gone.

Instinctively, I moved to follow; but Holmes clutched my arm. "No, we must attend to the woman."

With a quick nod to Wells, we rushed down the hall, past a confused Stringfellow in the lobby, and out into the cold air. As I noted earlier, the Nuñez home in Berkeley Square was not far from the Alpine Club. Our feet would convey us there more quickly than a hansom. And so with a blowing wind at our backs, we took off past the shops in Savile Row and zigzagged our way from Clifford Street to New Bond Street to Bruton Street and finally into the Square itself.

As we ran, Holmes pulled out the card Mrs Nuñez had given him containing her address.

"We have no precise idea what the man has planned," said he as we pulled up in front of a small terraced house of grey stone, "but I suspect we should not arouse the household when we enter."

No sooner had we reached the outer door than Holmes produced his lock-picking tools, and within seconds we were inside. No servants appeared, and I was about to leap forward, but again Holmes restrained me. Placing his forefinger at his lips, he signalled me to be silent.

Dark-blue velvet curtains had been closed to keep the house in darkness. None the less, we managed to tiptoe across the entry hall until we were facing a pale, hard-edged stone staircase. It was only then that I understood the nature of Nuñez's diabolical plot, a plot that Holmes himself had somehow already deduced. For that matter, it was only then that I understood the madman's final words to us: "Be careful not to wake her."

In spite of the gloom, I could just barely discern the lethal piano wire Nuñez had mounted at the top of the staircase some four inches above the penultimate step. The thin wire had been pulled taut between the two vertical rungs supporting the bannister rails on either side of the stairs.

At that moment, we heard a door swing open; and Mrs Nuñez, dressed in a white, silk dressing gown with her blonde hair askew, appeared at the head of the stairs. "Is someone there?" she called, moving forward at the same time.

"It is Sherlock Holmes, madam!" my friend shouted. "Do not move!"

She heard the name, but his command did not register.

"Mr Holmes?" she queried, walking forward all the while.

My friend bounded up the stairs just as the poor lady was reaching the wire. When her small, slippered foot encountered the obstacle, she let out a curiously mild "oh," and stumbled forward—directly into the arms of Sherlock Holmes.

*****

Would the fall have killed her? It is difficult to say. A week later, Holmes and I were still discussing the case. On this occasion, we were seated in our armchairs before the fire at Baker Street drinking the sherry that, thanks to Holmes's *charade* with the blindfold a few days earlier, I had never got to sample. As an ironic reminder of that madcap experiment, Holmes actually discovered the square of black silk with which he had covered his eyes. It was stuck between the cushion and the arm of his chair. He cocked an eyebrow and laid the blindfold in his lap.

"Recall, Watson, that Mrs Nuñez tuned pianos as well as played them. As a consequence, I assumed there would be any number of spools of the strong, thin wire lying about the place, a perfect tool for any number of different murderous acts—garrotting and hanging are but two examples. With such an idea in mind, I found Nuñez's remark about not waking his wife to be more predictive than cryptic. It suggested a plot still to be set in motion. If I was correct about the use of piano wire, perhaps the stuff had not yet accomplished its evil task."

Alas, Nuñez's motive was a hypothetical that would remain unresolved. All that we could conclude with any certainty was that, despite our alerting Scotland Yard to the villain's escape, Juan Carlos Nuñez was never found. No doubt, a man with his knowledge of travel possessed many a clandestine alternative for slipping aboard some ship bound for South America, the first leg of his return to the country of the blind. To this day, he remains unaccounted for.

On the other hand, we had little doubt that Mrs Nuñez, in spite of the obstacles she faced on a daily basis, would rebuild her life. In addition to the solace her music provided, she also retained the material properties Nuñez had left behind. As a blind woman who had learned to read Braille, master the piano, and move comfortably among the sighted, there was little reason to doubt she would continue to be successful in the future.

As for Bertie Wells, though neither Holmes nor I knew it at the time, it would take him another two years to write the adventure for which he had paid Nuñez so handsomely. Although Nuñez's notes never turned up—if they ever existed in the first place—Wells was able to construct a credible manuscript from what Nuñez had already told him as well as from—dare I say?—fabrications of his own making.

In 1904 H.G. Wells published the narrative he titled "The Country of the Blind" and in it depicted how life was lived in that hidden valley. The story related Nuñez's initial experiences among the sightless people and continued only until the time of his escape. "An adventure into the unknown—that is the part of Nuñez's tale that people want to hear"—or so Wells explained it. From a practical point of view, Wells left to me the task of writing the more pedestrian account of the mountaineer's escapades in London.

In contemplating my report of the matter, I realised that it was Nuñez's escape that galled me the most. Not only would the man responsible for all the grief escape an appearance in an English courtroom for attempted murder, but presumably he would also get to spend the rest of his days with the woman he loved. "Not fair at all," said I to Holmes.

"And yet, old fellow," Holmes assured me, "he quite literally faces a very dark future indeed."

"Reunited with his lover?" I countered. "Where is the darkness in that?"

"You forget, my dear Watson, the pre-condition of this second marriage—blindness is the price he is to pay." To emphasise the point, Holmes actually covered his eyes with the blindfold and tied it behind his head. "If Nuñez is to be believed, he is destined to lose his eyesight—a prospect once so terrifying that it had prompted him to risk his life in escaping from the valley."

Observing the blindfolded man before me made the judgement seem all the more real.

"It may actually be true," Holmes continued, "that in the country of the blind, the one-eyed man is king"—and here he raised half the cloth to expose a single steel-grey eye—"but let us not forget, old fellow, that unlike myself at this moment, Señor Nuñez will never be able to escape his newly inflicted world of total darkness."

I raised my glass to indicate my appreciation of Holmes's view of justice and then sampled my drink. At the same time, Holmes pulled down the silk so that it once more covered both his eyes. In spite of the blindfold, he had no trouble in bringing the glass of sherry to his lips, which at that very moment were curled into a self-satisfied smile.

An Adventure in the Mid-Day Sun

There was a desert wind blowing . . . . It was one of those hot dry
Santa Anas that come down through the mountain passes and curl
your hair and make your nerves jump and your skin itch. On
nights like that . . . meek little wives feel the edge of the carving
knife and study their husbands' necks. Anything can happen.
--Raymond Chandler
"Red Wind"

I

Cold summers make the warm days feel all the
hotter—the way the briefest of smiles from a frosty girl can
set a man's heart aflame. That's why the blazing sun in the
middle of the cool and wet July of '03 felt as if it were
blistering the city. You don't easily forget such lingering
heat, the kind that makes the roads shimmer and the horse-
droppings and petrol fumes stink; the kind that turns
drinking bouts into pub brawls; the kind that makes mild
folks contemplate mayhem. On such a day you enter the
street with an extra dose of caution; you regard all people
with a wary eye.

And yet that very heat seemed to make no difference
to Mrs Hudson. I may have been sweltering in my dark,
wool tunic, the one with the buttons forming a V down the
front; but even if the garbage did smell worse and the wool

115

did stick to my skin, she still commanded: "Billy, remove the trash."

A bit of history: As far as I know, all the page-boys who've ever worked at the house numbered 221 in Baker Street have been called "Billy". In point of fact, I was born "Ray Chandler"—"Raymond", to be more precise—fifteen years ago in America; but when I was seven, my mum brought me to England.

We visited family in Ireland and ultimately settled in London, where I enrolled as a day-student at Dulwich College. Like any other healthy lad, my mind began to wander; and having recently got into some trouble at Dulwich, I was "encouraged" to take a job during the little free time I had, summer months included. According to Florence Thornton Chandler—that is, my mother—I would have much less chance of getting into mischief if I kept busy.[*]

With Uncle Ernest funding my education, I didn't need the meagre pay a page-boy's job provided. But to show contrition for my earlier transgressions, I agreed to work in Baker Street for Mrs Hudson, who conveniently had connections, however indirect, to my mother. Conveying the odoriferous garbage outside on the hottest day of the year is only one of the many chores I perform for Mrs H. Sweeping floors, running errands, announcing visitors also keep me busy.

Not that I'm complaining, mind. No fifteen-year-old ever wants to waste his time working, but relatively speaking I'm quite happy with my position. What teener

---

[*] For details of Chandler's so-called misconduct, see Dr Watson's *The Final Page of Baker Street*. (DDV)

wouldn't want to be employed at the residence of Mr Sherlock Holmes, the world's first consulting detective? Especially if that teener wanted to be a writer. For Dr Watson, Mr Holmes's friend and biographer, frequently gives me suggestions concerning my own writing, advice that I have much appreciated since I regard his own work so highly.

I may have read Aeschylus, Marlowe, and Twain at Dulwich, but I still find especially appealing Dr Watson's true-life crime sketches that appear in *The Strand*—not to mention the sensational fiction of his literary agent, Arthur Conan Doyle. Even though Dr Watson recently left Baker Street to be closer to his medical practice, he does come round frequently enough to peruse the new compositions I set aside for him.

Such perquisites, however, provided scant comfort in the heat of that day in July. On such a day, even a priest might loosen his collar. And outside with the garbage in tow, the sun seemed hotter; my uniform, thicker; the dustbin, heavier. If all that wasn't bad enough, I still had to heft the bin's contents—in this case, the detritus of Mrs Hudson's fish and chips from the previous night—into the large metal garbage bin in the narrow alleyway. To my great disappointment, there weren't even any distractions like servants or other pages dumping their own refuse at the same time. The dusty cobblestone seemed all but deserted.

And yet I did catch a glimpse of one figure out back—though technically he wasn't actually standing *in* the alley, but lurking behind the corner of a neighbouring house. From what I could discern before he ducked behind the wall, he appeared to be a young boy dressed in baggy, black trousers torn at the knee and a loose-fitting, collarless white shirt. The idea that he might be peeking at *me* flashed through my brain; but as I could conjure little reason for such behaviour, I picked up the now empty dustbin and, giving the lad no more thought, returned to my duties inside.

I was passing through the entry hall when the front bell clanged. Wondering who might be visiting on so hot a day, I opened the outer door and was greeted by an enchanting vision, a handsome young woman of fair complexion whose dark hair was swept up in in the latest style. With her trim figure clothed in a dress of white cotton buttoned to her neck and wrists, she was quite the looker. But then, like a moth to the flame, I've always been attracted to women some years older than myself.

"Is Mr Sherlock Holmes in?" she asked, her face flushed from walking in the sun.

I nodded. "I'll announce you," said I and asked for her name, which she provided. She then followed me up the seventeen steps, and I knocked on Mr Holmes's door.

"Enter."

The white muslin curtains of the sitting room had been pulled back to allow a greater flow of air; and as a result, the room was bathed in sunshine. The reflection from the yellow-brick building across the road added to the brightness. Attired in his purple dressing gown, Sherlock Holmes sat in his armchair reading a newspaper and, despite the oppressive heat, smoking his black clay pipe. As usual, his books and newspaper cuttings lay at odd angles round the room—collections that, as I valued my life, I'd been instructed never to touch.

"Mrs Frank Barclay of Hampstead to see you, sir," said I in what I hoped was my most imperious tone.

With a wave of his hand, he signalled that I should show her in. The woman brushed past me as Mr Holmes replaced his dressing gown with a jacket. The two exchanged quick introductions, and I started to exit and close the door.

"No, Billy," Mr Holmes surprised me by saying, "leave the door open. It might help cool the room."

I shrugged and nodded, then slowly left to resume my chores.

"Billy," roared Mrs Hudson from downstairs. "The hallways!"

Now I know that Dr Watson's readers think of Mrs H as some sort of mother hen. But let me assure everyone that, though she might keep after Mr Holmes and the doctor in a maternal fashion, she can call out orders like a cawing gull to those that work for her.

Fortunately, sweeping the hallways included the landing in front of Mr Holmes's rooms—out of Mrs H's line of vision from the ground floor. Had I not been so isolated, I would never have been able to prolong my dawdling and, at the same time, overhear the woman's story.

"—string of valuable pearls stolen from my home in Hampstead," she was in the midst of saying when I returned with the broom, "and I would like *you* to find them for me, Mr Holmes."

Although I'd been employed at Baker Street but a few months, I'd seen enough of the great detective in his listening mode to picture him sitting in his soft chair, his back to the sunlit window so his visitor would see him in silhouette unable to read his expression. His eyes would remain half-closed, his fingers steepled together—almost as if he wasn't paying attention. But, of course, he was—like a serpent about to strike.

"The pearls were given to me by my former *fiancé*—"

"'*Former*'?"

"Phillip Stanley," said Mrs Barclay softly. "Perhaps you've heard of him. He drove racing cars and was killed in a terrible crash during the Paris-Bordeaux Rally a couple of years ago. It was horrible. We were to be married, and—"

An abrupt silence followed except for a few hiccupping sounds which I took to be the woman's sobs.

After a moment to compose herself, she continued. "Phillip gave me the pearls as an engagement gift. The clasp was fashioned to look like a pair of racing wheels, spokes and all."

"Quite so," murmured Mr Holmes.

"I first met Frank Barclay at one of Phillip's races. Frank was charming, and I was vulnerable following Phillip's death, and Frank and I ended up marrying the following year—no doubt, a mistake for both of us. Frank worked on French racing cars, you see, and frequently journeyed off to the Continent to attend races—among the other pleasures he fancied there. To facilitate my own travels during his absence, I hired a driver, a young fellow named Waldo Mackintosh who'd been recommended to me. But Frank is a jealous husband, Mr Holmes; and upon his return, he sacked the man. I won't deny that I may have given him reason to distrust me, but I certainly can find better companionship than a mere *chauffeur*."

I didn't know what Mr Holmes might make of such a confession; but with a woman as pretty as she, I could readily understand her husband's suspicions.

"Here's where the strange part begins," she continued. "Just before his departure, in what appears to be some sort of misguided revenge, this Mackintosh, the driver, made off with the necklace Phillip had given me. I thought I'd never see the pearls again, but yesterday the villain contacted me. He wants to sell the necklace back to me for one hundred pounds. A *hundred* pounds! They're beautiful pearls, but I don't think they're worth *that* much.

"I take it that you never had them appraised."

"No, Mr Holmes. I'd always planned to, but I never did."

"More's the pity."

"Then I thought of *you*. I'd heard that you handle such transactions, and I've come to ask for your help. In fact, if you'll forgive my boldness, I assumed you would agree. That's why I told Mackintosh to meet me here today."

Dr Watson has already reported how Sherlock Holmes represented a woman of honour in a similar situation. Mr Holmes had hoped to offer mediation between her and the conniving blackmailer, Charles Augustus Milverton; but the man's murder intervened. Only with Milverton's death and the destruction of his incriminating files could much of aristocratic London sleep more easily. Still, like the poisonous weeds they are, such villains have a way of coming back for more. As a consequence, I reckoned Mrs Barclay had come to the right man. Mr Holmes was—

"You, boy!" Mrs Hudson cried, poking a finger in my back. "Don't be lollygagging round Mr Holmes's door. Sweep up this hallway, and take the refuse outside. You know the way. We don't want to miss the dustman."

Leaning on the broom and listening to the woman tell her tale, I never heard Mrs H come creeping up on me. It didn't seem fair, her tiptoeing about like that. Nonetheless, within minutes I was traipsing back out into the hot sunlight, once again dumping refuse into one of the large, stinking bins.

Unlike my earlier venture into the alleyway, however, this time I discovered that I was definitely not alone.

II

Fists were flying some thirty feet down the alley. Despite the heat—or because of it—two combatants in black suits and black bowlers, one man pale, the other swarthy, were having at each other, shouting, shoving, punching. Suddenly, the darker of the two broke free and, extracting a small revolver from his jacket, fired off two quick shots. Both bullets found their marks, and the other man's hat flew off as he staggered backward, clawing at the air, then crumpling to the ground. The bowler, on the edge of its stiff brim, rolled a few yards away. It slowly spun to a stop and came to rest, right side up, near the corner of the neighbouring building.

The man with the gun used his foot to prod the inert form lying before him. There was no movement. Satisfied that his victim was dead, he snarled, "*Now* we're level," and stooped over to check the dead man's pockets. It was only after pulling out what looked like a packet of folded bank notes that he squinted up the alley and saw me gawping at him. My eyes must have been as round as a pair of Mrs H's fine-china tea saucers. Worse—baked by the sun, I couldn't move—not even when he raised the pistol in my direction and, pointing it at my heart, kept the barrel steady whilst marching toward me.

"Sorry, boy," said he breathing heavily. "No witnesses."

Fearing the worst, I shut my eyes, and I clearly heard the click of the cocking mechanism. I was sweating heavily now, and it had nothing to do with the heat.

I waited. And waited. But the gunshot never came; the pistol didn't fire. Instead, a new voice—a threatening whisper it was—greeted my ears. It was coming from behind my assailant.

"Hoy," it said with a cockney accent, "drop the rod, or your throat gets cut."

Unable to breathe, I opened one eye. To my great astonishment, I could see the boy with the baggy trousers positioned directly behind the shooter. He was pointing his blade into the gunman's neck. I'd originally reckoned him to be eight or nine, but from the way he was holding that long knife, I could tell that he was no young child. Though small in stature—undernourished perhaps—he had a large head, and he scowled fiercely as he pushed the blade harder against the man's soft flesh.

What the boy might actually have done had the shooter not conformed, I never asked. Thankfully, the man's icy demeanour turned to water, and a moment later I heard the clank of the revolver hitting the ground.

"Damn," the villain muttered to himself.

In an instant, I retrieved the pistol—a .44 calibre British Bull Dog, as Mr Holmes later identified it—and handed it to my rescuer, who now pointed the weapon at the man.

"I'll get help!" I cried. "Don't let him get away."

With that, I raced back into the house, past an open-mouthed Mrs H, and up the stairs. The door to 221B had remained open, and I burst into Sherlock Holmes's sitting room. He was still talking with Mrs Barclay, and he looked up in amazement at the interruption.

"Outside!" I gasped. "In the alley. A man's been shot! There's a boy out there aiming a gun at the shooter."

The detective jumped to his feet, excused himself to Mrs Barclay, and snatched up a small, shiny cylinder from the mantel. Then he rushed down the stairs and out into the blinding sun. I followed right behind.

"It's all right," I told the boy who was still pointing the pistol at the shooter. "You can give the gun to Sherlock Holmes."

A big grin crossed the lad's face, and he eagerly complied.

Holding the weapon in one hand, the detective raised a police whistle to his lips, for such was the object he'd grabbed from the mantel. A few short blasts followed. Then crouching low, he checked the pulse of the man on the ground. A moment later, he looked at me and shook his head. The poor wretch was dead. The scarlet pool spreading beneath the body underscored the fact.

With the gun still trained on the shooter, Mr Holmes proceeded to riffle through the pockets of the dead man. Finding nothing, he now turned towards the assailant and indicated with a flick of the gun that the man turn out his own pockets. Flashing an angry scowl, the villain produced a dirty white handkerchief and a cheap cigar broken at the centre. Reluctantly, he also revealed a handful of neatly-folded ten-pound notes—no doubt, the same notes I'd seen him steal from the dead man. Holmes took the money and secured it inside his coat.

At the same time, the heavy beat of running footsteps announced the arrival of a uniformed constable.

"Mr Holmes," the winded policeman managed to say, "What's the trouble?" The constable obviously knew the detective.

"Clamp the handcuffs on this man, Dalmas. Then notify your superiors. I'll take him inside and keep an eye on him until they arrive. I leave *you* to deal with the body here."

"Right you are, sir." He touched his forelock as if he'd been talking to Mr Balfour himself and proceeded to secure the metal bracelets round the prisoner's wrists. They fastened with a reassuring click, and the constable strode off to complete the rest of his assignment.

Sherlock Holmes marched the shooter past Mrs H, who by now was used to such goings on in her establishment, and back up the stairs to his sitting room. Mrs Barclay, who'd moved to a corner, started when she saw the villain.

"Excuse the disturbance," Mr Holmes said to his visitor, "but in my line of work, interruptions like this sometimes take precedence."

"Of—of course," she said with less conviction than her words conveyed.

"Stand by the door, Billy," he commanded, and I took up the position as instructed—though uncertain what I would do if the fellow tried to bolt.

As if he were hosting the villain for tea, Sherlock Holmes offered his shackled prisoner a chair not far from Mrs Barclay. Perhaps it was the lady's calming influence, but the bloke seated himself without incident. More likely, it was the pistol, whose butt end could be seen peeking out of the front pocket of the detective's coat. Mr Holmes paced up and down the sitting room as he addressed the man.

"Your name, sir?"

"I don't mind telling you my name or my business," the former gunman said proudly. "I'm Al Teasel, and in a

125

different day I might have been called a highwayman. But that bloke had it coming. Worked a job with me, didn't he? We got caught, and he peached to the police, blaming it all on me. *He* walked free whilst I was four years in the nick. When I got out, I reckoned I'd settle the score. I spent months looking for him and almost gave it up. But then today—quite by accident, really—I spied him in Marylebone and followed him here to Baker Street. When he finally saw me, he ran into the alley. You know what tempers are like in this kind of heat. I guess you might say he made a fatal mistake."

"And what, pray, was the name of your unfortunate victim?"

"Waldo Mackintosh," spat out Teasel.

In the corner, Mrs Barclay gasped. "Mackintosh? Why, he's the man I told you about, Mr Holmes. My former driver—the one who stole my necklace. He must have been bringing it here to sell just as I'd asked." She stood and walked over to the detective. "Did you find any pearls on his person?" she asked him.

"The dead man was carrying nothing," said Mr Holmes, who now turned and fixed his grey eyes on Mackintosh's killer.

"Don't know nothing about no pearls," Teasel admitted, "but I grabbed the seventy pounds that was in his pocket—the same seventy *you* just took from me."

"Which I'll be giving to the police," Holmes advised.

Mrs Barclay shook her head. Word of the dead man's empty pockets had obviously crushed her hope of reclaiming the pearls that meant so much to her. She extracted a linen handkerchief from the end of her sleeve and dabbed at her eyes. But even so, she couldn't prevent the tears.

A heavy tread on the stairs interrupted the scene, footfalls announcing the arrival of the police. They turned out to belong to the moustachioed Inspector Youghal, the same policeman I'd first encountered when Mr Holmes settled the matter of "The Mazarin Stone".

"The body's on its way to the morgue," Youghal greeted us, pulling at his thick moustache. "Just as well. I wouldn't want to be spending any time with a corpse on a scorcher like today." Eying Mrs Barclay, he added, "Beggin' your pardon, Madam."

It took but a few moments for Mr Holmes to explain matters. The inspector copied into a small notebook the name of the victim and, placing in an envelope the seventy pounds Teasel had been holding, slipped the notebook and envelope inside his coat pocket. The inspector then placed a hand on the prisoner's shoulder, turned him toward the open door, and escorted him down the steps and out into Baker Street. Once Teasel exited the building, a uniformed constable carefully secured him inside the police van that had been standing by the kerb.

A lad doesn't get the chance to see a murderer herded into a Black Maria very often—especially not where I lived in quiet Dulwich—so I was quick to follow Mr Holmes and the others outside. At the same time, I also couldn't help noticing the boy that had saved my life. In all the excitement, I had forgotten about him, and yet there he was, peering over a garden wall at me from less than a hundred feet away. Despite the macabre nature of the day's events, he was smiling beneath the dead man's bowler. It fit his big head perfectly.

III

"That tall gent—that was really Sherlock 'olmes, the detective?"

The van had clattered off down the road, and the others had gone back inside. The boy and I were standing in the sun a few paces from the front door.

"Yes, indeed," said I, puffing out my chest. "I work for him. I'm the page-boy here at 221."

"I know that, mate," the boy surprised me by saying. "It's why I've been following you, hain't it?"

I stared at him in light of his curious comment. He took off the bowler, and I could see that he wore his dark hair neatly combed. Torn trousers or not, he was a handsome lad with sharp, piercing eyes and an engaging smile. What's more, as I suspected, he appeared not as young as I'd previously thought, but rather closer to my own age, perhaps a trifle younger. Now that he was no longer skulking in the background, he seemed friendly enough; and beneath his humorous exterior I sensed a kind of sensitivity as well.

"What do you mean, 'following me'?" I challenged.

This question produced a laugh. "I'm an actor, hain't I—a stage actor. I'm about to join a theatre company what's putting on a play titled "Sherlock 'olmes". We're going to tour the country—might even get up to Scotland."

"Go on," I scoffed, "you're just a kid. And Sherlock Holmes is a man."

The boy giggled infectiously. "Are *you* thick!" he cried. "I hain't the detective; I'm still the kid. I play the part of Billy the page."

"Billy the—" I began. "Wait a bit. That's *me*!"

"Right you are, mate. Which is why I've been following you. I'm studying up for my part, hain't I? If I'm good enough, maybe I'll end up on a stage 'ere in London."

"Wait a bit," I said again. "You know *I'm* Billy. What's *your* name?"

"I'm Billy too, hain't I?" said he with a grin. "Billy the page." And he repeated that winsome laugh.

"You're a regular comic, aren't you?" I shot back, my tone full of sarcasm. Practical joking wasn't designed for sweltering afternoons. "What are you really called?"

"Charles Spencer Chaplin," he smiled. "But m' friends call me Charlie."

"I don't know," said I, figuring it was my turn to prod. "You look a mite small for a role as important as Billy's. Maybe you're not big enough for the job."

I should have known better than to joke around on a day like that. Hot weather makes people do crazy things. The smile dropped from his face as, reaching down in his pocket, he produced the long knife he'd held at the throat of the gunman. Only this time he pointed it at *me*.

"This blade says I *am* tough enough. Been brought up in the streets, 'aven't I? See fights all the time. Though I must say, guns hain't usually part of the mix. What was that business with the shooting all about?"

I put up my hands in mock surrender. He'd saved my life. He deserved to hear the details, and so I filled him in on all that I knew, right up to and including the lamentations of Mrs Barclay, who'd lost her precious pearls.

"Why don't we fetch 'em for 'er then?" asked Charlie.

I snorted. "Where would we look? Where would we start? We don't even know where the dead bloke came from."

"*I* do, don't I? On my way over 'ere, I seen 'im walk out of a boarding 'ouse—Fremont 'ouse in Gloucester Place it was—just the other side of Marylebone." Charlie put his hand on my shoulder. "Let's go."

I glanced at the front door. "But Mrs Hudson—my job . . . ."

"Your job's to 'elp Sherlock 'olmes, hain't it? Let's give 'im a 'and by finding the pearls for the lady."

Maybe it was the heat, but I couldn't muster the energy to argue. Besides, he was right. It was very much my job to aid Mrs Hudson's boarders, Sherlock Holmes included. And so without a look back, I joined up with Charlie Chaplin, who'd replaced the bowler at a rakish angle atop his head. With the thrill of the hunt leading us on, we made our way to Gloucester Place and the rooms of the late Waldo Mackintosh. If I'd known what we were about to find, I might have been less eager.

IV

The original red brick of Fremont House was bleeding through the whitewash, and the black paint on its weather-beaten outer door was peeling in the heat. Worse, it was locked. As we stood at the entrance wondering how to proceed, the door was pushed open from the inside by a gent sporting a boater.

Charlie tried to slither in behind him, but the fellow used an arm to block his way.

"Here now," the man said. "You can't just go rushing in like that."

"Please sir, we're looking for Mr Mackintosh, m'uncle," said Charlie, hat now in hand, eyes wide, voice—minus the Cockney accent—tinged with innocence. Quite the actor was my new friend; there was no denying his persuasive manner. "M'dad's a carpenter, and he's cut his pinkie clean off. He needs m'uncle's help. D'you know what room he might be in?"

The man nodded. Whether or not he believed Charlie's story, the matter appeared not the sort to get him riled up about while baking in the sun. "Room four," said he, and he even held the door open for us. As soon as we were in, Charlie plopped the bowler back on his head.

"What if we get caught and somebody tells your dad?" I asked in the foyer. I could just imagine how angry my own mother would be down in Dulwich if she found out that her son had been sneaking into the digs of some poor bloke who'd been murdered—especially since I'd been sent to Baker Street to straighten out my evil ways.

"*My* dad?" repeated Charlie with a snort. "'E won't care. 'E's been dead for two years, hain't 'e? I never saw 'im much anyway—though 'e did start me clog-dancing on the stage. I do owe 'im that."

There was a boiling stuffiness to the ground floor where a single charwoman was listlessly dusting a white-pine sideboard in the sitting room. She showed little enough interest in us, so up the stairs we climbed. We found the room we were seeking on the first floor. The corridor itself was dark, but we managed to read the faded numbers painted on the doors.

Charlie placed his hand on the doorknob and turned.

"Locked," he whispered. "But not to worry." From inside a pocket he pulled out a set of small metal picks. "One of these should work." And sure enough, like a jeweller tinkering with a clock, he got the tumblers to fall and the door to open.

A ripe aroma instantly hit our nostrils, no doubt the stench of some food gone bad exacerbated by the heat. But we had a job to do, and so we covered our noses with our forearms and entered. A faded-red curtain covered the rear half of the room, the flimsy cloth setting off the sleeping area. A small window on the back wall let in enough light for us to see though, owing to the curtain, everything seemed bathed in a scarlet wash. Fortunately, the place was small, and we calculated that our search shouldn't take long. The area in front of the curtain contained only a wooden table, two cane-back chairs, wall-pegs for hats and coats, and a chest of drawers. The curtain itself concealed the bed.

"You look for the pearls back there," Charlie commanded, pointing in the direction of the curtain. "I'll check the bureau," and he yanked out one of the two top-drawers.

"Quiet," I cautioned.

Since there was so little furniture in the room, the worn curtain and what it might be hiding seemed to offer the greatest mystery. With the smell growing fouler as I approached and hesitant at what I might discover, I slowly drew back the thin red cloth. As it turned out, I had good reason to be concerned.

A large hook for a chandelier was fastened to the ceiling near the left-hand wall, no doubt a remnant of the building's more refined distant past. In this instance, however, it wasn't a lighting fixture that hung from the hook, but a black leather belt whose nether end was strapped tightly round the neck of the poor soul dangling below it. Clad in a worker's brown overalls, the hanging man clearly looked dead. With bloodshot eyes protruding and tongue coloured blue extending from between his teeth, such a conclusion seemed obvious. Beyond the noose-like belt, I could make out purple bruises at his throat. I'd learned enough from Sherlock Holmes to figure out that the man had been strangled before he'd been strung up.

"Ch-Ch-Charlie," I managed to say.

But he ignored me. Instead, he shouted, "Look 'ere!" and held up a string of white pearls in one hand and a stack of fat envelopes in the other.

He flashed a broad grin until he glanced over my shoulder and saw the grisly scene I'd just come across myself. Then his eyes grew wide.

"Let's get out of here!" he cried.

It was fine with me. Shoving the pearls and envelopes inside his shirt, Charlie checked that the hallway was clear, and then we both bolted down the steps, slowing up only long enough not to distract the char. She was still dusting half-heartedly in the afternoon heat.

V

When Charlie and I arrived back at Baker Street, Sherlock Holmes was sitting in his shirtsleeves by the open window and smoking a cigar. We were bursting to give him our report about the dead man in Fremont House, but he held up his hand to silence us. He closed his eyes and, reminiscent of the American Indian who sends puffs of smoke into the sky to signal his mates, blew a great white cloud towards the window. When he finally got round to focusing his grey eyes in our direction, it wasn't to question us concerning our discoveries but rather to ask me about my companion—that is, the boy who'd saved my life.

I was hoping to blurt out the story of the dead man! To scream the news of the pearls and letters we'd found! But I knew enough about Sherlock Holmes to understand that following *his* way of doing things ensured the greatest chance for success. And so in spite of the developments I longed to report, I ended up relating how Charlie had come to my rescue in the alley when Teasel had pointed the gun at me. My new friend and I had pressing information to impart, and yet Mr Holmes appeared more interested in learning that Charlie was a budding actor in a drama about the detective than in hearing what we had to tell him about the case he was working on.

"I am familiar with Gillette's play that bears my name," he said, his voice full of disdain. "It is a waste of dramatic effort." But then he added wistfully, "You know that I myself trod the boards a number of years ago. Even now I employ many of the techniques I learned in the theatre." He exhaled another cloud of smoke, this time into the room itself.

I understood full well the techniques Mr Holmes was referring to, for I'd read Dr Watson's descriptions of the various disguises the detective continues to utilise. And yet, sweltering as I was, I knew that those counterfeit dotty vicars and bent old ladies and grimy labourers would have to step aside. I could contain myself no longer.

"We found the pearls!" I exploded. "Mrs Barclay's pearls! Charlie knew where Mackintosh lived, and we went there, and we found the necklace and a pile of envelopes filled with letters. And there was a dead man in the room."

"A dead man? Letters?" Mr Holmes carefully placed his cigar in the ashtray next to his chair and leaned forward.

I told him about sneaking into Fremont House and the body hanging in the room and how Charlie had discovered the necklace and the envelopes in Mackintosh's bureau.

"We'll have to notify the police," Mr Holmes murmured; but even whilst uttering these words, he extended his open palm and motioned with his fingers that we hand over the necklace. Charlie pulled it out from somewhere inside his cavernous shirt and gave it to me to hand over. Mr Holmes frowned as soon as I laid the pearls in his palm. The closer he brought them to his eyes, the more quickly the frown turned into a scowl.

"The clasp is just like the racing tyres Mrs Barclay described," he observed, "and yet these pearls aren't real. A passable imitation, perhaps, but nowhere near as valuable as Mrs Barclay had suggested. I am amazed that it actually fooled her."

"Show him the letters," I told Charlie. Fishing inside his shirt again, Charlie produced the envelopes he'd taken from Mackintosh's room. Out shot the detective's palm once more, and this time Charlie himself filled it with the envelopes, through which Mr Holmes immediately began to thumb.

"Standard stationery. Postmarked in London. Addressed to Mr Barclay in a woman's hand. Written in cursive English, the dotless i's suggesting Russian training. Other than the sender's address on Sumner Place with no name given, there's nothing particularly noteworthy about the envelopes. Now let's look inside."

Mr Holmes proceeded to examine the letters themselves. He even sniffed the pages. A few minutes passed before he announced: "One doesn't need the aroma of perfume to infer that these letters to Mr Barclay are from a Russian lady. They suggest an intimate relationship about which neither the writer nor the recipient would want Mrs Barclay to know. I can only assume that just as Waldo Mackintosh had stolen the pearls from Mrs Barclay, so he must also have stolen these compromising letters from her husband. Quite a resourceful brigand, the late Mr Mackintosh! Unless I'm greatly mistaken, he had plans to extort money from wife and husband at the same time without either one of them knowing about the other."

The detective stood up and took his coat from the rack.

"Come, " said he, looking in my direction. "We shall pay a visit to the return-address on the envelope. It is time to meet Mr Barclay's lady-friend."

I pointed at Charlie. "*Both* of us?" I asked hopefully.

The hint of a smile crossed the detective's face, and he strode to the open door.

"Mrs Hudson!" he called down the stairs.

Within minutes Mrs H appeared, arching an eyebrow when she caught sight of me standing in the room.

"Here, Billy," said she, brushing away a strand of her grey hair that had come unglued in the heat. "Where have you been all afternoon? There's work needs to be done."

I exchanged glances with the detective. "I was engaged on personal business for Mr Holmes," I dared to say, hoping he'd support me.

In fact, he went a step further. "Actually, Mrs Hudson, Billy has been most helpful. As has his friend Charlie here. And I was wondering if you might do us a favour."

He proceeded to describe Charlie's upcoming role in the play about Sherlock Holmes. Though he told little about the details of the drama, he emphasised the importance of her Baker Street residence in the story and suggested how much more accurate the production might be if Charlie could be given an actual uniform and allowed to spend a short time performing as a page-boy in the real Baker Street rooms.

"Oh, I should be honoured," said Mrs H smoothing down her dress as if she too might be stage-bound. "I'll be right back."

She returned a few minutes later with a smaller version of the uniform I was wearing and handed it to Charlie.

"Ta," said he before going downstairs to change. Minutes later he re-appeared in the guise of a Baker Street page.

"You look swell," I greeted him. "Now 221 has two 'boys in buttons'."

Charlie looked down at himself and straightened his jacket. "This feels good," he said with a smile. "In m'old rags I felt like a tramp—even with that bowler I recently acquired."

In spite of his new uniform, however, I knew that Charlie wasn't satisfied. I understood that not being removed from an actual murder case meant more to him than learning the role of page-boy. But I needn't have worried; Mr Holmes had another job in mind for him. The detective had not yet notified the police regarding the hanged man Charlie and I had discovered at Fremont House. Appreciating Charlie's desire to be included, Mr Holmes now wrote a note detailing the matter and handed it to him.

"Give this to Inspector Youghal at Scotland Yard and to no one else," Mr Holmes instructed. "This information is very important. The police will know it's authentic when they see you in Mrs Hudson's livery."

It didn't matter to Charlie that he was already sweltering in the new wool tunic. He had an important service to perform. His eyes sparkled and his smile beamed; and like a soldier receiving an honour, he straightened out his uniform, clicked his heels together, and offered a small salute. Then he was off.

"Come, Billy," Mr Holmes said to me. "You and I shall travel to the address listed on these letters and see what we can learn about Mrs Barclay's husband."

VI

Though it was not surprising to discover that the Old Brompton Road in Kensington was just as hot as our own front steps in Baker Street, it was indeed a surprise to encounter Frank Barclay himself in the small flat in Sumner Place.

As it turned out, no servant answered our ring. A plain but heavily made-up young woman dressed in yellow cotton opened the door. Giving her name as Irina Glukhov, she turned out to be none other than Mr Barclay's lady-friend. As Mr Holmes had surmised, she was Russian.

A tall, portly man in shirtsleeves was standing behind her. When he heard who was calling, he donned a coat and joined the woman at the door.

"I am Frank Barclay, Mr Holmes," said he perspiring freely and offering no hand to shake. "I suppose my wife Emily hired you to snoop on me. Well, you found me out. Can't say I'm pleased to see you, but I suppose I will be rid of you more quickly if I speak to you now."

In spite of such seeming openness, neither he nor the woman made any effort to invite us to sit down. Rather, the four of us remained bunched together in the stuffy entry hall, as if Mr Barclay might usher us out at any moment.

Indicating his companion, he said, "I met Irina during a car race in Paris. I'm an automotive engineer and was working on a Mors."

"Ah, yes," Holmes nodded. "'The Mors Machine'. A V engine configuration, if I remember correctly."

"Quite impressive, Mr Holmes. Actually, it is a V4 side-valve. And though I could talk about such a racing car the entire afternoon, I assume that the Mors is not the point of your visit."

"Quite so."

"Well, mine is not a complicated story," Mr Barclay said, mopping his brow with a linen handkerchief. "Irina agreed to accompany me back to London. I got her this flat, and I spend a great deal of time with her—more time now than I do with my wife." He squeezed her shoulder as if to confirm his commitment.

Mr Holmes and I exchanged glances. My personal sympathies were obviously with the wronged Mrs Barclay.

"You are aware that Irina's letters to you are missing?" asked Mr Holmes.

"Alas, I am." Mr Barclay raised his eyebrows. "Do you know their whereabouts? I'd hidden them at the bottom of a desk drawer, but obviously not well enough. At first, I thought that Emily had found my hidey-hole. But when I heard nothing from her about them, I supposed they must have been stolen. In point of fact, I feared contact from a blackmailer."

"Any one blackmailer in particular?"

"Why, I don't know what you mean."

"I think you do, Mr Barclay. I think you suspected that the man you sacked not long ago, Waldo Mackintosh, your wife's chauffeur, had stolen your letters. So much did you believe it that you sent one of your employees— possibly a mechanic, judging from the description of his work clothes—round to Mackintosh's rooms in Gloucester Place to buy them back for you."

"The seventy pounds Teasel stole from Mackintosh!" I exclaimed.

"Yes, Billy. Mr Barclay here gave a man in his employ seventy pounds to buy back the stolen letters from Mackintosh."

"He's a French mechanic called Leon Grimaud," added Barclay. "And, actually, I paid him twenty pounds to complete the deal. The other fifty was Mackintosh's price for the letters themselves."

"Then this Grimaud," I remembered, "must have been the dead man in brown overalls."

"Dead man?" Barclay cried, eyebrows arched. He mopped his brow once more.

"Quite dead," answered Mr Holmes. "One can only assume, Mr Barclay, that the twenty pounds you paid the late Mr Grimaud wasn't enough for him. The man had obviously wanted more."

"Wait a moment," said Barclay, a wrinkle crossing his brow. "If Grimaud is dead and Mackintosh ended up with Grimaud's money as well as the money for the letters, how come I never got the letters back?"

"Really, Mr Barclay," the detective replied. "I believe it is no less a figure than Falstaff who complains that there is 'No honour among thieves'. Mackintosh stole the money out of the pocket of the man he'd just killed. Perhaps Grimaud paid out the fifty pounds, plotting to kill Mackintosh himself and steal it back. More probably, Mackintosh suspected Grimaud's murderous plan from the start and simply stole the money after strangling him."

"The bruises on the hanged-man's neck," I said. "Right, Mr Holmes?"

"Yes, Billy. A misguided attempt to make Grimaud's death look like suicide. Of course, we'll never learn exactly what happened since both men are dead."

"Mackintosh is dead too?" Barclay gasped, his face turning ashen.

"Oh, I neglected to inform you. Shot by an angry confederate late this morning, a fellow named Teasel."

Barclay took a deep breath, and his nostrils flared.

"The police are investigating both murders, Mr Barclay. They know about the money, but not about the letters. I am the one who has those."

Barclay now patted his lips with the linen. "May I have them back?" he asked. "Or do I now have to pay *you* for them. I don't want any trouble with Emily. While I'm sorry to hear of Grimaud's death—Mackintosh's too, for that matter—they have nothing to do with me. I never gave orders for anyone to be killed."

"It's strange," said Mr Holmes coldly, "but I believe you. And yet such a conclusion does not exonerate the contemptible treatment of your wife." The detective reached into his coat, produced the stack of envelopes and handed them to Mr Barclay. "I am returning to you all of your letters save one." And here he patted his breast pocket.

"You will receive the remaining epistle once I am informed by Mrs Barclay herself of the satisfactory disposition of your marriage. She is my client, and I shall accept whatever resolution she prefers.

"Come, Billy," said Mr Holmes as he turned to the door. "We have yet another stop to make."

I thought we would be off to the Barclay home in Hampstead, but Holmes had the hansom drive to Golders Green where we stopped at a jeweller's shop. He told the driver to wait, and I followed the detective inside. A tiny bell above the door jingled when we entered.

Seated behind the counter and looking up at the sound of the bell was a bespectacled man with a greying beard. He wore a black skullcap and a white shirt open at the collar. I don't know much about gems and stones and such, but most of the gaudy pieces I saw within the glass cases looked like the kind you can win at some game or other on the Brighton Pier. A chessboard lay at the end of the counter. The game has always interested me, but these pieces stood in random fashion. A bishop lolled on its side as if too enervated by the heat to perform.

"Mr Lazarus," said Holmes, clearly having done business with the man before, "in very short order I need you to put together a necklace much like this one." From his coat pocket he produced the pearls we were soon to return to Mrs Barclay, the ones that had been stolen by Mackintosh. They shone in the sunlight that was pouring through the window and heating up the place.

The jeweller took out a lens and examined the necklace. After a few moments, he leaned back and removed his glasses. "Ah, Mr Holmes," he sighed, "Bohemian glass beads. A good reproduction, perhaps, but in the end, still a fake. I could easily create for you a necklace of false pearls, but mine would look significantly cheaper than this one."

"Precisely my wish."

The old man shrugged and replaced his glasses. Then he opened a drawer and scooped up a handful of tiny white balls. They could have been glass marbles.

"And, Lazarus," Holmes added before the jeweller got to work, "in the piece you are now making, be sure to include the clasp from the necklace I just gave you."

I looked at Mr Holmes questioningly whilst the old man nodded and disappeared into his workroom somewhere behind a wall at the rear of the shop.

"When we visit Mrs Barclay," said Mr Holmes, "I will offer her the cheaply-made necklace. She will easily identify it as a poor imitation and not the one that was stolen from her. I will then inform her that Mackintosh had sold what she thought was her 'valuable' original and was planning to give back to her a cheap imitation in its place."

"But the original was also a fake."

"Yes, Billy. *We* are privy to that information, but she is not. Recall that she said she'd never had the opportunity to appraise it. She still thinks it real. Why inform her now that the gift given to her by the late Mr Stanley, the man she loved so dearly, was just a handsome imitation? This way, she'll believe that Mackintosh sold away the cherished original and planned to fool her with a cheap replacement. Her romantic memory of Mr Stanley will remain intact."

I could see nothing wrong with the plan—nothing besides the fact that it undermined the common belief that Sherlock Holmes lacked sentiment. For what it was worth, I nodded my approval.

The jeweller reappeared and laid both necklaces in long, black rectangular cases. Mr Holmes gave the man some money and collected the boxes. I followed him out of the shop, the little bell ringing again as soon as the door was opened. We resumed our seats in the hansom as it rattled off down the Finchley Road.

The Barclays lived in a small house in Hampstead not far from Heath Street. Holmes again asked the driver to wait, and within moments a housekeeper was opening the door and ushering us into a simply furnished sitting room. Like everything else that day, the house was hot; and as in 221B, the curtains had been pulled back to expose the open windows. In this case, however, there was the shade of oak trees just beyond the walls to help lessen the heat. Within moments, Mrs Barclay joined us, and we rose to greet her.

"Would you care for some tea, Mr Holmes? For you and your young man."

"No thank you. I am here on business, and then I must return to Baker Street."

"Pray, sit down then and tell me the worst."

"It was as I feared, Mrs Barclay," he said. "The pearls originally given to you by Phillip Stanley have been replaced by these poor imitations." He handed her the box containing the newly made false necklace.

No sooner had she opened the box than a sneer formed on her lips. "These don't look anything like mine!" she exclaimed.

Holmes pointed at one end of the strand. "You will notice that Mackintosh retained the original clasp, the racing tyres."

"As if these odious pearls could fool me," she muttered. But then she brought the necklace to her bosom.

"I shall save the clasp. It is all I have left to remind me of Phillip. This trash I shall discard."

"Then our job here is done," said Sherlock Holmes as he rose to his feet. "I trust that Mr Barclay will soon contact you and that some measure of calm will descend upon your household. I informed your husband that I am expecting to hear from you directly about the resolution of your marital differences." Glancing at me, he said. "Come, Billy."

Mrs Barclay escorted us to the door. Holding it open, she watched as once again we climbed into the hansom.

"To Baker Street!" Mr Holmes shouted to the driver.

VII

No sooner did we enter the outer door at 221 than the siren sound of laughter beckoned. It emanated from the kitchen, and it was there that we discovered Charlie sitting at the wooden table opposite Mrs H, who was roaring with delight. Charlie had jabbed a pair of forks into a couple of dinner rolls and, keeping his head low to the table top, was using the forks to manipulate the rolls. They appeared to be the dancing shoes of a very short body attached to Charlie's very big head. He turned his face this way and that, arched his brows, and—with an exaggerated smile, smirk, or grin—presented many the hilarious expression to accompany the mincing steps. What an entertainer! Mrs H was laughing so hard that her eyes disappeared behind the rounds of her cheeks, and even Sherlock Holmes provided an appreciative chuckle.

"Quite a show!" I cried. "It would be even funnier with musical accompaniment. Try one of Scott Joplin's rags."

Charlie nodded; but in spite of Mr Holmes's quick smile, seriousness had entered the kitchen alongside the detective, and within a minute the uproarious entertainment came to an end.

"Your report, Charlie?" Holmes asked.

Charlie confirmed that he'd personally delivered to Inspector Youghal the note about the hanged man; and while Charlie and I polished the silver tea service for Mrs Hudson, I furnished him with the details of the afternoon's activities.

Charlie worked at perfecting his performance as a Baker Street page-boy until it was time for him to leave town a few days later with the *Sherlock Holmes* touring company. I can say with great sincerity that I was sorry to see him go and not—I hasten to add—just because he'd lightened my workload.

*****

It would be two years before we laid eyes on Charlie Chaplin again, two years during which a number of major transitions occurred. First and foremost, Mr Holmes retired to a cottage in the Sussex Downs. I myself left Mrs Hudson's service to devote more time to my studies in Dulwich. As for the Barclays, they agreed to an uncontested divorce and went their separate ways.

Charlie re-entered out lives at the Duke of York's Theatre in the late fall of 1905. In point of fact, he left tickets for Mrs Hudson, Mr Holmes, Dr Watson and me to an evening performance of William Gillette's play, *Sherlock Holmes*. By then, the drama that Mr Holmes once derided

146

had gained international acclaim. We all knew of the favourable reviews though none of us—emphatically *not* Mr Holmes—had actually seen a production. To honour Charlie, however, even the detective agreed to take advantage of the boy's largesse and journeyed up from Sussex that very day to join us for the performance. He met Dr Watson at his home in Queen Anne Street, and the two of them had their four-wheeler stop in Baker Street where I had joined Mrs H. Together we all drove to the theatre in St. Martin's Lane.

Anticipating an enjoyable evening, everyone looked pleased, everyone except Mr Holmes.

"Publicity annoys me," he muttered when, above the clatter of the carriage wheels, I questioned his dour expression.

"Oh my," sighed Dr Watson. "Here we go again. I can assure you that I've heard the same complaint regarding Holmes's appearances in my own sketches. Be forewarned, Billy, should you ever write your memoirs and attempt to include Sherlock Holmes."

Mrs H nodded in support of the doctor.

"The more people who recognise me," said Mr Holmes, "the harder the job of detecting becomes. Anonymity is key in my line of work."

"He does have a point, Doctor," Mrs H said, now in agreement with the detective.

"You too, Mrs Hudson?" said Dr Watson, "I think the man doth protest too much. They say that this chap Gillette has captured you perfectly, Holmes. They say you have much to be proud of."

"'They *say*, they *say*'," muttered the detective to no one in particular. And he hunkered down against the back cushion like a limp boxer retreating to his corner of the ring.

Soon we were walking past the delicate arches, powerful columns, golden fittings, and burnished wood of the Duke of York's Theatre on our way to the stalls. I wound up sitting on the aisle with Dr Watson to my immediate left; and once the lights dimmed and the red velvet curtain rose, I could see the good doctor nodding in expectation.

Dr Watson became even more energetic in joining the thunderous applause that greeted William Gillette once he strode onto the stage. Erect and noble, the actor smoked a golden-brown calabash; and though it was a style of pipe that I myself had never seen among those on the mantel of 221B, even Mr Holmes flashed a smile.

We all grinned approvingly at Charlie's performance as Billy the Page. Obviously, the time he'd spent learning my job had paid off handsomely. He could tug at his tunic and announce a visitor with professional ease. Just then, Dr Watson nudged me and gestured to the left in the direction of Mrs Hudson. At that very moment, she was displaying a broad smile in recognition of the very same uniform she'd given to Charlie.

For all the doctor's enthusiasm, however, I must say, that when the amiable Kenneth Rivington, the Dr Watson of the piece, came charging onto the stage, my neighbour started sputtering.

"See here," he whispered, grabbing my arm. "That fellow's nothing at all like me."

"It's merely a *charade*, sir," I reminded him.

But the doctor couldn't be placated. "These actors are a cantankerous breed. Their imaginations have run amok. They confuse fiction with reality."

Perhaps he was right—though such ambiguity doesn't bother *me*. In terms of my own writing, I don't let the issue of reality get in the way. Labels like "interesting" or "dull" mean more to me than questions of "fact" or "fiction". Take my personal situation as an example. Personally, I never considered my housekeeping chores at Baker Street as noteworthy, but here was the audience in the Duke of York's watching a boy in buttons make mundane labour seem attractive. Obviously, there is much in one's personal experiences that can entertain an audience.

Suddenly, I found myself thinking about stories that might be fashioned from events in my own life. What happened to my father after he'd run out on my mother and me in Chicago? Who was responsible for the dead body floating down the muddy river near my aunt's house in Nebraska? What was prompting Uncle Ernest to pay for my education in Dulwich? With a few pokes here and a few pokes there, I might even fashion a mystery tale in the tradition of Dr Watson or his agent, Arthur Conan Doyle.

I'd need to create my own consulting detective, of course; one couldn't expect a mere page-boy to get involved with murders on a regular basis. But at least I was beginning to espy the genesis of a plot or two. For that matter, a writer could do worse than base a narrative on the two-year-old murder in the alleyway behind 221. Ignited by a blistering, red-hot summer's day, the type with which everybody is unfortunately familiar, the tale contains a kind of universality. After all, unless you reside at the North Pole, who hasn't lived through one of those scorchers?—the sort of day that renders the bullet or the blade the simplest of solutions, the sort of day that is so hot that just about anything might happen . . . .

The Adventure of the Star-Crossed Lovers[*]

Why should the world be over-wise,
In counting all our tears and sighs?
Nay, let them only see us, while
We wear the mask.
--Paul Laurence Dunbar
"We Wear the Mask", 1896

Marriage is one of the "basic civil rights of man," fundamental to
our very existence and survival . . . . [T]he freedom to marry, or
not marry, a person of another race resides with the individual and
cannot be infringed by the State.
--U.S. Supreme Court,
Loving v. Virginia, 1967

I

*W*hether one calls it the most disheartening mistake
of my career or simply the most foolish, it is I who has had
to live with the terrible consequences. The origins of the

---

[*] With great appreciation to Samuel Williams, Jr., whose novel
Anomalous was first to bring together two of Conan Doyle's more
memorable characters, Lucy Hebron from "The Yellow Face," and
Steve Dixie from "The Three Gables." (DDV)

woeful tale actually date back to the early spring of '88; but the more immediate events, those that led to its tragic conclusion, began one bright summer's afternoon in early July of 1903. I was returning home to Queen Anne Street following an afternoon in my club and thought I might stop in at my former rooms in Baker Street to visit my friend and colleague, Mr Sherlock Holmes.

Generally, Mrs Hudson welcomed my appearance. Today, however, with lips sealed in a straight line and arms folded across her chest, my former landlady eyed me with suspicion. Standing tall and firm in the entry hall a few feet from the outer door, she displayed an undisguised look of disapproval as I passed; and she continued to mark me even after I had mounted the stairs.

As it turned out, a client occupied my friend's sitting room. Not surprisingly, Sherlock Holmes was seated with the windows behind him. In daylight hours, the stratagem served to cast Holmes's face in silhouette, concealing his facial expressions from the person positioned opposite him. However effective in masking his reactions, such placement also served to present the back of the client to anyone entering the sitting room from the hallway, thus shielding the visitor's identity from view.

Upon arriving, therefore, I discovered my own powers of observation severely limited; all I could determine with any certitude was that Holmes appeared engaged in conversation with a young woman. I could not distinguish her facial features, yet her composed voice and gestures, not to mention her fashionable green frock and small, single-feathered hat, clearly indicated a person of substantial breeding and refined upbringing.

"Ah, Watson," said Holmes, rising to his feet, "allow me to introduce an old friend."

I had no idea to whom Holmes was referring, but I must confess to being all the more astonished when the young lady in question turned to face me and I perceived the chocolate hue of her skin. I am ashamed to admit that I froze in my tracks, mouth agape, beginning to understand the critical look in Mrs Hudson's eye. Though many a peculiar type had marched up the seventeen steps to Holmes's lair over the years, few had been female, and even fewer had been black.

"An-an old friend?" I stammered.

"Miss Lucy Hebron," Holmes announced.

"Miss Lucy Hebron?" I repeated mindlessly.

"Watson, Watson," Holmes admonished, "have you forgot our investigation in Norbury of the girl with the yellow face?"

The Yellow Face. Norbury. Suddenly, it came back to me. Fifteen years before, Holmes and I had attempted to resolve the mysterious comings and goings in that town of an Englishwoman called Effie Grant Munro. Holmes had got it wrong at first and seemed unable to put his error out of mind. Indeed, he suggested that whenever he might appear too full of himself, I should "kindly whisper Norbury" in his ear to bring him back to earth.

Fortunately, it had not taken long for Holmes to right the problem. The woman's strange behaviour, which had prompted Effie's husband to call upon my friend in the first place, had been part of a ruse to conceal the arrival of her daughter Lucy. The little girl was the product of the woman's earlier marriage to one John Hebron, an American Negro lawyer of Atlanta where Effie herself had grown up. Hebron had died from yellow fever when Lucy was very young; and Effie returned to England, leaving the little girl, who had also been struck down by the illness, to be cared for in Atlanta by a former servant.

Though Effie remarried and became Mrs Grant Munro, she soon found herself longing for her daughter. Yet fearing an angry reaction from her new husband towards the black little girl, she requested the child be sent to her in secrecy. What is more, to deter recognition, not only did Effie have her daughter cared for in a nearby cottage, but she also required the child to don a yellow mask whenever the girl approached a window.

Fortunately, the matter was happily resolved. Indeed, Holmes and I took great comfort in the tolerance that Grant Munro displayed in accepting the child into their household. I shall never forget how, after first meeting his black stepdaughter, he lifted her in his arms and kissed her. For the moment, it actually gave one hope for a future in which diverse peoples might live together in peace, an optimism I sought to recreate in the sketch I titled "The Adventure of the Yellow Face".

Obviously, the little black girl had blossomed into a beautiful young woman. She had been but a child when I first set eyes upon her; and yet I suddenly realised that during the years that followed, I had never encountered a black personage of my own social set—not to mention so charming an example. In hope of adapting my manners to a situation that was new to me, I asked, "What brings you here, my dear?" and tentatively offered my hand.

She took it up immediately. "Oh, Dr Watson," said she, "it is indeed wonderful to see you again—although, truth be told, I was too young to remember the occasion of our first meeting." She smiled in my direction, but seemed to catch herself and averted her eyes. Unless I was very much mistaken, it was not a happy circumstance that had brought her to Holmes's door.

"Before your arrival," said he, "Miss Hebron was in the process of telling me the fears she harbours for her *fiancé*. Why not lend an ear, old fellow? Your advice in matters romantic has always proved invaluable."

Compliments from Sherlock Holmes never failed to move me; yet I must also admit that, flattery aside, I was especially interested in hearing what a young lady from our past might have to say. I settled into an armchair while Holmes returned to his own seat and invited Miss Hebron to resume her story.

"As I told Mr Holmes, I am recently engaged to a fine gentleman called Josiah Fipps. He works as an accountant in the City for the banking firm of Westmoreland and Franks. We met whilst admiring the roses at Kew Gardens."

"Charming," I observed.

A smile flickered in the young woman's face though it took but a moment for a frown to replace it. "I suppose," said she, "I must also add that he is white."

In spite of the shocking nature of their mixed relationship, that last bit actually went without saying. One could not imagine a long-standing institution like Westmoreland and Franks daring to place the funds of its white clientele in the hands of a Negro.

"Mr Fipps and I are quite used to receiving hostile looks and the odd remark when we appear together in public. But one develops a thick skin in reaction to such offensive behaviour and learns to go on about his business. Which is not to say that such hostility doesn't cause great distress."

"Of course," said I, knowing full well that as a white man myself I could not possibly comprehend the depths of her pain.

"Once we announced our engagement, however, matters worsened."

Holmes brought his fingers together in their familiar steeple. "In what way did they worsen?"

"First, there was the rock thrown through the window of Josiah's flat."

"A rock, you say?" I asked.

"With a note tied round it."

Holmes leaned forward in anticipation. "Did you bring the note with you?"

I could easily envision him, lens in hand, analysing the paper, the ink, and the handwriting.

"Alas, no," replied Lucy Hebron. "It was so offensive that Jos burned it in the grate. I do, however, remember its foul language."

If ever one seeks similarities among diverse people, one need only recall the sad look in their eyes when they recount the words of insult hurled at them.

"It said, 'Stay away from niggers'"—Lucy flinched at repeating the hateful epithet—"'lest you be treated like one yourself.'"

Holmes and I exchanged looks of grave disapproval.

"What else?" he prompted.

"Jos told me of a similar letter delivered to him a week later," Lucy frowned. "It arrived at his office in Lombard Street. Sorry, Mr Holmes. He destroyed that one too—right away, in fact, so it wouldn't be seen by any of his colleagues. Jos is not naïve, gentlemen. For that matter, neither am I. We recognise the disgust with which many people regard our companionship—let alone our engagement. For that reason, Jos has refrained from announcing our upcoming nuptials at work, but neither are we shying away from the news."

"Surely," said Holmes, "for two strong individuals like Mr Fipps and yourself, there must be more that brought you here than just those two ugly notes."

"Indeed," nodded Lucy Hebron. "I still live with my mother and stepfather in the house you visited in Norbury all those years ago. One afternoon not long after the rock and letter incidents, I was leaving home to visit a friend when a closed four-wheeler that had been waiting nearby tore down the road in my direction and suddenly veered into my path. I tell you, gentlemen, at that instant, I feared for my life; but at the last moment, the driver, his face concealed behind a black scarf and wool cap, pulled the horses back to the centre of the road. It had rained earlier that day; and fortunately the only pain I suffered was the humiliation of being splashed with the mud that had collected in the roadway."

"Outrageous!" I cried.

"Could you identify any marks about the carriage?" Holmes asked

Once again, Lucy nodded. "I recognised the name of Chadwick's on its door. It's the local stables in Norbury. Anyone in the world might have hired it, and so I let the matter drop." Her voice dropped as well, her report apparently finished. She now sat staring at the two of us biting her lower lip.

"And yet, Miss Hebron," observed Sherlock Holmes, "I sense there is still more to tell. As unsettling as the events you have described must be, they occurred weeks ago. What has happened just recently that has finally brought you to my door?"

Lucy Hebron reacted to Holmes's question with silence. She had kept her hands gently folded in her lap when recounting her story; but now she raised them and, entwining her fingers, clasped them tightly together. A single sob escaped her lips.

"Take your time, my dear," said I softly and actually found myself leaning forward and placing my pale palm atop her dark hands.

The young woman threw back her shoulders as if to gain strength. "Jos was beaten by thugs," she hissed. "Sunday last when we walked through St. James's Park. We came upon three young men who, once they'd seen us, pushed me out of the way with some foul words and then set upon Jos. 'No nigger lovers here!' they screamed at him. One held Jos from behind, and the other two took turns hitting him."

The account sickened me, and I vaguely recalled a sentence from *Huckleberry Finn,* the American novel about racial intolerance—something about being "ashamed of the human race."

"This must stop, Mr Holmes!" demanded Lucy, her voice full of defiance. "That's why I have come to you. Jos doesn't know I'm here. He tells me not to worry; he says we simply have to get used to the malicious acts of ignorant people."

"Yes," Holmes intoned, "your Jos does have a point. One cannot set about correcting the foibles of everyone in the world."

Lucy arched her eyebrows. "*Foibles,* Mr Holmes?" she cried. "Is that all you can think to call these happenstances? Mere *foibles?*" Her eyes grew wide, their whiteness standing out in contrast to her dark skin. "I expected such a reaction from the *police.* That's why we never bothered to report the incident. But I did not anticipate so tepid a response from *you,* sir. My parents have always spoken of Sherlock Holmes with the greatest regard. In fact, it is why I have called upon you today."

"My apologies," Holmes said, leaning back in his chair. "Perhaps you misinterpret my meaning."

On more than one occasion, I have referred to my friend as an emotionless reasoning machine. I am afraid that his unfeeling reaction to the complaints of Lucy Hebron typified his aloofness.

"White skin, black skin," he proclaimed, waving a hand in the air, "they mean nothing to me when compared to the human brain. To express emotional concern over such distinctions is to minimise the power of thought. The most brutish of white men can stoop as low as any black, just as the minds of both races can soar. To paraphrase the Bard, 'what a piece of work is man, how meaningless his colour'. I have no patience for such distinctions when the game's afoot. It is the villainous perpetrator I seek regardless of his skin's hue. The word 'Negro' conveys nothing more to me than does the horse of that name that ran against Silver Blaze in the Wessex Cup."

Holmes did well in citing a previous case. It served to put me in mind of a corroborating comment he had made while investigating the Cunninghams of Reigate back in '87. "I make a point of never having any prejudices," he had said on that occasion, "and of following docilely along wherever facts may lead me."

However truthful Holmes's speech to Lucy Hebron, the lady's shoulders sagged at its conclusion. "Perhaps I've expected too much," she sighed. "Maybe the intolerance I have observed typifies *all* white people, and my mother simply serves as a notable exception. She and my true father had to leave Atlanta, you know, because of the ignorant and prejudicial laws there.

"Even before the yellow fever struck, they were planning to come here. I think they believed that the British people had a reputation for greater understanding—at least, compared to that of most Americans. After all, Britain ended the slave trade some thirty years before the American Civil War."

"Quite so," I was pleased to agree.

"To illustrate the point even further," Lucy went on, "after I had recuperated and finally arrived in Norbury, my mother and later my new stepfather provided me with private tutors and generally sheltered my upbringing. As a little girl, I never had reason to doubt the wisdom of their decision to live in England. And yet, with all the Negrophobia I've seen in the last few months, I'm no longer certain that the British reputation for tolerance is deserved."

It pained me to hear my race so severely denigrated, especially by such an innocent voice. "Do not disparage the British, Miss Hebron," I countered. "As you noted, we may indeed have our own shameful record of slavery, but we are a people that can rise above it. You yourself have grown up here and are testimony to that fact."

"Watson is right on that score, Miss Hebron," said Holmes. "Let me put my mind to it. Something doesn't ring true regarding these events. I shall visit you in Norbury tomorrow afternoon to explain my reasoning; and I trust that, schedule permitting, Dr Watson will join us."

"I certainly hope you *will*, Doctor," said Lucy Hebron.

Need I hear more? Naturally, I would attend the gathering. Not only was British honour at stake, but my personal reputation as well. John H. Watson made it a habit of never turning down the request of a stately young lady in distress—no matter, I had only now just discovered, the hue of her skin. Breeding, money, grooming, colour—in my mind, all are trumped by beauty.

Holmes's old friend Maupassant put it this way in his story, "The Diamond Necklace": "Women belong to no caste, no race, their grace, their beauty and their charm serving them in the place of birth and family." In fairness, however, the desire for justice had also to be included as one of the essential attributes of the young lady seated before me.

"Of course, I shall be there," said I, confident that in the name of supporting victims of prejudice, my wife would raise no objections to my venture.

A smiling Lucy Hebron rose to her feet, and Holmes and I stood as well. To Holmes, she said, "For whatever light you may shed on this matter, sir, Jos and I will be truly grateful."

"I shall see you to a carriage," said I. No need to let the charming Miss Hebron have to face the critical eye of Mrs Hudson unescorted.

It was the thought of the landlady that prompted yet another realization on my part. In spite of the tolerance shown by Mrs Hudson towards Holmes's odd behaviours—the bullets shot into the wall, the chemicals fouling the air, the bust in the window luring an assassin—one could not divorce this kind lady from the cultural assumptions of our age. However little Mrs Hudson may have intended it, her otherwise benign and stoic attitude actually provided cover for the very acts of cruelty and violence described by the latest client of Sherlock Holmes.

I boldly offered Miss Hebron my arm, and down the stairs the two of us marched, past the centurion of a landlady and out into Baker Street.

In addition to the summer's heat, the usual *mélange* of rattling carriages, shouting merchants, stinking horses, and jostling pedestrians filled the air. In my mind, the act of accompanying the young lady to the kerb amidst the chaos seemed the gentlemanly thing to do. Yet to my great surprise, it turned out to be much more than that—or so I learned as Miss Hebron broadened my understanding of social indignities.

"Thank you for coming along with me, Doctor," said she. "If a white man like yourself signals for a cab, they usually stop. When a black man or woman tries, they frequently drive right past."

I had never bothered to consider the privileges of being white. There was, I now realised, a lot more I had never considered and much more that I had always taken for granted.

*****

By the time I climbed back up the stairs, the sitting room was clouded with pipe smoke. Holding his favourite briar, Holmes sat in his armchair, knees propped under his chin.

Fixing me with his intense grey eyes, he said, "Consider, Watson—the rock, the letter, the splash of mud—they all occurred when the principals were alone. Only the beating took place when they were together. Does that not evoke an immediate conclusion?"

"Only the commonality of prejudicial behaviour," said I angrily, my thoughts still pondering those final words of Lucy Hebron.

"Of course," said Holmes with a dismissive wave of his pipe. "What I'm referring to is the strategies involved. For the rock and the letter to reach their destinations, whoever delivered them had to know the home and business addresses of Mr Fipps. And the devious carriage that almost ran down Miss Hebron—whoever rented it had been waiting for her near her home. Once more, someone knew where to find her."

"Agreed," said I, "though now that you bring it up, the attack in the park seemed unpremeditated. Unfortunately, the poor couple stumbled upon a band of prejudiced street-toughs."

"Exactly, Watson! Unless I am greatly mistaken, one must conclude that, unlike the assailants in the park, whoever sent those notes to Fipps and whoever pointed that carriage in the direction of Miss Hebron are quite familiar with the habits of both personages. It is a subject I intend to explore more fully on the morrow during our visit to Norbury."

With that cryptic pronouncement, he placed his pipe on the mantel, bade me good day, and—violin in hand—retired to his bedroom.

II

The late-morning train to Surrey deposited Holmes and me in Norbury not long past noon the following day. A few more shops than I had remembered now populated the area surrounding the railway station. One in particular,

Chadwick's Equestrian Equipment and Carriages, caught Holmes's attention.

"A moment," said he, as we were about to set off for Pollards Hill where the Grant Munros lived. Before I could respond, he disappeared within the confines of a freshly painted red wood-barn. Not long thereafter, he emerged with a look of satisfaction. Motioning me to join him, he murmured, "As I had expected," and marched on.

Within minutes we found ourselves on the same rustic road that had led us to the little black girl and her yellow mask more than a decade earlier. Like the new shops in the village, more cottages now appeared along our route. Though numerous groves of yews and beeches and rolling pastures of green forage continued to dominate the scene, there could be little doubt that the forces of progress were beginning to overtake the pastoral countryside. It could not be more than a few years before additional roads and structures would be vying for prominence.

Soon we were passing the cottage in which little Lucy had been secreted away and then we were turning down the tree-lined lane that led to the handsome, two-storied villa of Grant Munro. (I valued it at eighty-pounds-a-year the first time I saw it.) But here too the isolation was receding. On the road above Munro's villa, a few more cottages had joined the two I remembered near the inn.

Holmes gave the entrance bell a pull; and though the door was opened by the same Scottish woman who had appeared ancient so many years before, she was immediately supplanted by the master of the house. His hair now tinged with grey, the still muscular Grant Munro ushered us into the sitting room where the principals in the drama were awaiting our appearance: his wife Effie, their daughter Lucy, and a clean-shaven, clear-eyed, straight-shouldered man whose bruised cheeks informed us that he must be Josiah Fipps, Lucy's recently victimised *fiancé*.

Upon our arrival they rose in unison, but Grant Munro quickly motioned for all to resume their seats and offered Holmes and me the two empty wing-chairs that faced the others.

I should say from the start that besides the greying hair, neither Grant Munro nor his wife had changed much since we had last seen them. Oh, there were a few more lines in their faces; but for the most part, the challenge of bringing up a child of colour in the midst of a white population seemed not have to undone them.

Grant Munro selected a long, amber-stemmed briar from a crowded wooden pipe rack. With two distinctive silver bands, the pipe appeared to be the same one to which he had been so attached upon our first meeting. He offered us tobacco, but we declined—in Holmes's case a sure indication that he wanted to move directly to the matter at hand.

"About these threatening notes," Holmes began.

"Damned haters!" Grant Munro cried out.

Effie placed a hand on his arm. "Jack, please allow Mr Holmes to continue."

Grant Munro tightened his jaw, but said nothing more.

Sherlock Holmes now repeated the inferences he had previously shared with me—that, given the fact that the threatening messages were delivered to known addresses, the writers must have been relatively familiar with either Lucy or Josiah or both.

"Nonsense!" cried Grant Munro, springing to his feet. "No one close to either one of them could have been responsible for those hateful messages. *No one!*"

A furrow darkened Effie's brow. "Jack, please," she said again. "What Mr Holmes has said makes perfect sense. Perhaps he may even have someone particular in mind."

Holmes bowed his head briefly. "Thank you, madam. Indeed, I do." He looked up at Grant Munro who had commenced the nervous pacing with which we were familiar. "Mr Munro," said Holmes, "it would be easier to proceed if you were to sit down."

Still seething, the man took his seat.

"Now, sir," said Holmes directly to Grant Munro, "I must ask you: for what reason did you hurl a rock through the window of Josiah Fipps's flat and send a threatening letter to his place of work?"

"Good God," I murmured as everyone's eyes turned to the head of the family.

"Mr Holmes!" cried his wife.

Grant Munro's face grew red; but he maintained his composure and gently set his pipe in a nearby ashtray. "I don't know what you're talking about, Mr Holmes. Certainly, you cannot believe that I, a man who accepted this wonderful girl as my own daughter all those year ago, could possibly have done anything at all to thwart her future happiness."

Lucy appeared too shocked to smile at her stepfather's compliment.

"So I too thought at first," replied Holmes. "After all, I was present the day you first met Lucy and embraced her with a fatherly kiss."

"A beautiful scene," I recalled. "I too remember it well."

"But then," Holmes continued, "I considered the matter more deeply. Take that dangerous carriage that almost ran Miss Hebron down. Why would its driver turn away at the last moment if he had truly set out to commit mayhem? If such a violent encounter had actually occurred on the wet road, if the carriage had in fact struck her, the event might well have been dismissed as an accident. Clearly, in this case there was no intent to harm. My doubts were confirmed when I described you to the proprietor of Chadwick's. He told me that although the person who had rented a four-wheeler on the day in question had swathed his lower face in a black scarf, the man's half-concealed features might indeed fit the description I offered. The stranger's money was plentiful, however, and the proprietor ignored any attempt to penetrate his mask."

As Holmes constructed his argument, Effie Grant Munro's eyes widened, and Josiah Fipps furrowed his brow. But it was poor Lucy, the victim of the aborted assault, who produced the tears. They trailed slowly down her dark cheeks.

A minute of silence ticked by. At last Effie spoke. "Have you nothing to say for yourself, Jack—you who once chastised *me* for underestimating your courage in matters of colour?"

Grant Munro, who had been looking down, now turned to Lucy and Jos. "I'm sorry," he said in a tremulous voice. "I was trying to spare the two of you the pain that always accompanies such experiments in social upheaval. I saw what your mother had gone through in seeking to protect you, Lucy—the lies, the fears, the machinations. How she secured a second house, how she kept from me her clandestine activities, how she allowed our own marriage to teeter precariously."

"Indeed," I said to Lucy, "your stepfather was quite upset when he visited Holmes and me in Baker Street all those years ago."

Grant Munro wiped at his eyes. "I was trying to save you from an ordeal you know nothing about, dear Lucy." He tried to secure Effie's hand, but she pulled it back from him.

"I've heard this tired history before, Father; and I appreciate all you had to put up with to keep our family together. But Jos and I love each other; and as far as we're concerned, nothing else need be said."

Jos gripped Lucy's hand. "It is our love," he proclaimed, "that will give us the strength to fight whatever bigotry comes our way."

"Like the attack in the park?" Grant Munro countered. "I had nothing to do with *that*; and unlike the results of *my* meagre warnings, the two of you suffered greatly."

Holmes nodded again. "I *assumed* that the assault in the park was random. Sad to say, such acts must be anticipated. If the two of you proceed in the direction you seem to have charted, I should imagine more of the same will occur."

"And yet that is precisely our intention," said the dark-skinned young lady, "to proceed—as you put it—in the direction we have already charted."

Her *fiancé* placed his arm round her shoulders.

Effie's nostrils flared as she beamed with pride at her daughter. "I should have expected nothing less," said she defiantly.

Grant Munro shook his head. "If you insist on placing yourselves at risk," said he with a note of resignation, "then I must remind you of a most significant fact."

Lucy extracted a white linen handkerchief from the cuff of her shirtwaist. Dabbing at her eyes, she asked suspiciously, "What is it?"

"A year remains before you reach your majority," said her stepfather. "Until that time, the law requires parental approval for someone of your age to wed. Grant me this one request. All I ask is that you take that time to examine your decision. If in a year from now you still wish to proceed, then you will have my blessing—my approval would no longer be needed—as well as a most generous wedding gift. Is that so great a sacrifice? I simply want what is the best for the two of you."

Lucy and Jos exchanged questioning glances followed by mutual shrugs. As best I could judge, it seemed that both of them deemed the proposition reasonable—if not desirable.

"A year seems a long time to wait," Lucy offered coldly, "but if it will make you happy, Father, I suppose we could manage."

With an accommodation in sight, Holmes took the opportunity to add, "I have no wish to interfere with anyone's personal considerations, only with the logistics of safety during the waiting time." To Lucy, he offered, "Allow me to find you protection, Miss Hebron." To her stepfather, he charged, "*You* will, of course, be asked to pay for such a service, Mr Grant Munro. But successful hops-agent that you are—not to mention the catalyst for so much consternation—producing money for such activity should not result in any major inconvenience."

"I cannot imagine that it should," he smiled. "Indeed, I relish the opportunity."

"Good!" cried Holmes with a clap of his hands. He obviously had some sort of plan in mind. "I shall communicate with you once I have arranged the matter. As for the conflicting passions aroused within your family, I trust you will resolve those issues among yourselves."

With those final words, Holmes got to his feet. I followed; and the two of us, offering the briefest of farewells, took our leave. In the railway carriage on our return to London, Holmes sat silently contemplating his next move.

*****

As I am certain the readers of my past works are aware, Sherlock Holmes, his claim of objectivity notwithstanding, displayed conflicting attitudes towards the question of race. On the one hand, confirming his view of the trivialities of racial distinctions, he could speak approvingly of Grant Munro's early acceptance of black little Lucy. On the other hand, he could just as easily hurl demeaning epithets at people of colour when he deemed such language useful. Among the more disquieting aspects of Holmes's character that I have reported, the insults he aimed at the Negro pugilist Steve Dixie just the previous May rank among the lowest.

Based on the boxer's reprehensible behaviour, Holmes could easily have limited his denunciations to the man's devoted allegiance to the criminal class. As I reported in the case I titled "The Three Gables", Holmes had voiced general suspicions regarding not only some "dirty work" Dixie had undertaken for the notorious Spencer John gang, but also a vague connection to the murder of a young man named Perkins outside the Holborn Bar. Yet instead of confining the basis of his disparagement to Dixie's criminal acts, Holmes preferred to insult the villain he called "Black

Steve" with various racial stereotypes. To cite but a few of his jibes, I offer Holmes's derogatory jibes concerning Dixie's smell, woolly hair, and large lips.

Due to their antagonistic history, it was to my great surprise that when I called on Holmes the following day, I discovered the huge frame of the very villain in question ensconced at Holmes's table in the Baker Street sitting room. Dressed in a charcoal suit with grey and red pinstripes and sporting a loud yellow tie, Dixie appeared less aggressive than I had remembered. On the contrary, employing his tongue to roll a toothpick between his teeth, the one-time boxer sat listening quietly to my friend.

"She's one of yours, after all," Holmes said to him. "I should think you'd want to protect her."

"That I would, Masser Holmes. Which is why I'm payin' so much attention to you." The toothpick was now still. "It's not everyday that old Stevie gets offered a noble proposal from the likes of yourself—not with the money to back it up, at any rate. No, indeed."

"Excellent!" cried Holmes, handing the man a small piece of paper. "Here is the address in Norbury. During daylight hours you are to keep at a discreet distance from the house. You will wait for the lady in question, Miss Lucy Hebron, to emerge—either on her own or in the company of her *fiancé* or parents—and then follow her about, intervening only when you sense she might be exposed to danger. At night, you may assign one of your associates to relieve you."

Steve Dixie removed the toothpick. "Long as we're paid, Masser Holmes," said he, offering a wide grin that showed off his white teeth, "I vow that my mates and me will do right by the lady."

Holmes proceeded to draw out of the breast pocket of his coat a number of pound notes. "These should do you for a while," said he as he laid them on the table. "I'll forewarn the family of your presence. Now get to work."

With the toothpick once more nestling between his lips, Dixie picked up the bills and examined them. Then with a nod, he inserted the money, along with the Norbury address, into a light-brown, kid-leather wallet and slid the wallet somewhere inside his coat. "Gentlemen," said he, addressing us both as he rose, "it's been a pleasure doin' business with you, I'm sure."

With that, he set a tweed flat cap on his head and, tilting his chin up, thrust forward the toothpick like the bowsprit of a frigate and stalked out the door.

"Perhaps you'll make an honest man of him after all, Holmes," I offered.

"I have come to understand, old fellow," my friend responded with a quick smile, "that developing one's character is sometimes simply a matter of gaining an opportunity to prove one's worth." With a dry chuckle, he added, "Time will tell."

III

One can only strive to do one's best in this cold-hearted world. Success is never guaranteed, and yet during the next few weeks I found myself longing for good news from Norbury. With the threatening messages from Grant Munro stopped at their source and the posting of a bodyguard in the form of tough Steve Dixie, Holmes had done all that he could to insulate Lucy Hebron from the benighted society that surrounded her and her man. And yet we heard nothing from the young woman.   Daring to hope that no news was good news, I found myself wondering whether Grant Munro's yearlong time-line for inter-racial harmony might actually be shortened.

The more days that passed, the more I wondered. And why not?   Did a union like the one between Lucy Hebron and Josiah Fipps not offer the next logical step in helping eradicate communal prejudices?   Before witnessing such a courtship involving people I actually knew, I had always deemed so idealistic a relationship as very far-off indeed, the kind of social harmony I would more readily expect to encounter in the fantasy world of my friend Mr H.G. Wells and his time machine than in the much more traditional landscape of Dr John H. Watson.

The desire to take action burned within me, and I found myself unable to wait any longer. Right or wrong, I decided, I would push the matter along on my own.   There was no need to raise the issue with my wife—"Don't meddle, John," I could hear her saying—or even with Sherlock Holmes, whose disapproval would be obvious.

On the final Saturday in July, therefore, I found myself sans my old friend on the late-morning train to Norbury.   Whatever the outcome, I was determined to involve myself in the personal plans of the Grant Munro family.   I hoped to prod Miss Hebron into fixing a specific date for her marriage—a date, I should emphasise, to be much earlier than the one her stepfather had mandated—in short, a date not far from the present.   To that end, I had sent a wire to Miss Hebron and Mr Fipps requesting a meeting that afternoon at the Munro villa.

In retrospect, I judge that it is at this point when one should raise the question I posed at the outset—foolish mistake or grievous error?   For my part, I can only say that the closer I got to Norbury—the train ride took less than an hour—the more strongly I felt possessed by the desire to make the very heavens smile upon this union. How, I wondered naively at the time, could anyone of right mind not be pleased with my effort to improve the human condition?

I sprang from the train at the station and fairly bounded down the road to Grant Munro's cottage. As expected, I espied Steve Dixie, toothpick in mouth, surveying the house from behind the trunk of a plane tree across the road.

"How goes the watch?" I enquired, tipping my bowler.

"Right as rain, Doctor," said he, offering an informal touch to the brim of his flat cap. "That is, once this Grant Munro bloke explained to the copper who kept sniffin' round just what I was doin' out here day after day."

I understood. "Not too many blacks milling about in Norbury, I should judge."

"Yeh," Dixie snorted, "none that *I've* seen anyway—besides Miss Lucy, that is. But there's so few houses out this way that there ain't too many *white* folks around to complain about me neither."

Bigotry again. Never before had I contemplated the extent of its pernicious omnipresence—never before had I felt the need. It was everywhere. Now, prompted by my little chat with Dixie, I felt my intentions even more confirmed, and I approached the house with a greater sense of urgency.

Fipps and Lucy were waiting for me. Assuring them that the black boxer would follow close behind us, I convinced them to join me in a short walk through the countryside. In the shade of the beech trees that arched the road, I hoped to convince the pair of the logic in marrying quickly. However presumptuous my suggestion, it seemed to me the appropriate action for them to take.

"Do you really think we should?" Lucy pressed me.

"Listen to the man," said Fipps before I could answer. "Dr Watson makes a valid point. Why worry about the artificial walls set up by the older generation? I love you, Lucy; and God knows we'll have lots more imposing barriers to surmount than the arbitrary timeline created by your stepfather."

Lucy smiled at her *fiancé* and clutched his hand. "Like Juliet's love for Romeo," said she, "my love for you is infinite. The more I give, the more there remains for me to give anew." Out on the open road, beneath a cathedral of arching branches thick with dark-green leaves, she dared kiss him on the cheek.

Romeo and Juliet indeed, I mused, quite enjoying the moment.

Suddenly, a wagon filled with hay came rumbling by. Its driver, an aging farmer with white side-whiskers, stared at the couple. As beautiful as had been Lucy's words, the old man, obviously repulsed by this display of affection between members of a different race, scowled and spat into the dirt. I saw Steve Dixie approach and then fall back as the wagon disappeared behind a bend in the road.

Lucy's focus would not be deterred by an act of ignorance. "We've been asked to wait," said she, "but there is also the law. How can we marry without the permission of my parents?"

Here was an opportunity for human progress, and I hoped to stimulate it as much as I could. In point of fact, I had anticipated Lucy's question and was ready with an answer. "There's Gretna Green," I offered, evoking the name of the southernmost Scottish village on the old coach road between London and Edinburgh. For years, the town had been the destination of many young English couples seeking immediate weddings. Unlike English law, the Scots required no parental approval, only two witnesses—the villagers themselves were generally eager to volunteer—and a twenty-one day residence requirement to be fulfilled by either member of the nuptial party.

"What a wonderful plan, Doctor!" cried Fipps, his speech quick with excitement. "Business is slow, and I should be able to make the journey immediately."

"Are you certain, Jos?" asked Lucy, a look of concern furrowing her smooth, dark brow.

"Westmoreland and Franks have already promised me time off," Fipps declared. "I'll travel to Gretna Green and come back for you in three weeks."

Clasping his hands in hers, the young woman closed her eyes. She must have been imagining their dream come true. Opening them again, she turned to me. "Oh, thank you, Doctor Watson. You've made me the happiest girl on the planet."

*****

The rest of the story requires but a few words of summary. What need is there to dwell on misery? For more than a month, neither Holmes nor I heard a word from the couple. One day in September, however, not long before Holmes retired to his bee keeping in the South Downs, I received a note to meet him in Baker Street. It was a solemn face he presented as he reached for the gasogene and prepared brandies for the two of us. Years before, Grant Munro had come to this very room and engaged Holmes with his own tale of woe. Today it was Holmes's turn to relate its latest permutation.

Just as I had envisioned, or so he told me, Lucy did indeed meet Jos in Gretna Green where the two were married. A blacksmith and his man served as witnesses. Once wed, the couple returned to Norbury where, thanks to Fipps's earnings, they managed to purchase a small cottage not far from the railway station. Grant Munro admitted that at first he had been outraged by the headstrong action of the lovers; but during the next few weeks Effie, appealing to the goodness in his nature, persuaded him to welcome the newlyweds into their home once more.

Would that the rest of the community had acted with the same magnanimity. As far as Scotland Yard could determine, one terrible night not three weeks after the fateful marriage, Steve Dixie's man was set upon by unknown assailants and knocked unconscious. These same vicious thugs then proceeded to set fire to the couple's house and escape into the countryside.

Fortunately, both Jos and Lucy were able to awaken, but so overwhelming was the smoke that it quickly threatened to overcome the pair. Only the young man's strength enabled him to save his bride. Though weakened by the noxious fumes, he managed to stagger away from the burning structure with Lucy in his arms and stumble to safety. It grieves me to say, however, that the smoke had done its damage. Not long after setting Lucy on safe ground, poor Jos, having inhaled too much of the thick, foul matter, expired in front of the smouldering remains of their cottage.

And still the tragedy had not fully played itself out. For Effie Grant Munro had never completely forgiven her husband's initial intimidation of the young couple.

Vanquished by grief, she gathered up her distraught daughter and within the fortnight following the fire left her husband and returned with Lucy to the unfriendly but familiar confines of Atlanta.

"Playing Cupid is never easy, Watson," observed Sherlock Holmes. "I thought you would have learned by now. The role is laced with an irony one frequently overlooks. All too often, what appear to be comforting scenes of love serve to mask the hidden but circumscribing rules of logic. In this case—neither the first nor the last, you can rest assured—it was the stringent demands of society that undermined the union of two lovers—" (here Holmes paused to sip his drink and offer a sad smile) "—not to mention any attempts at correcting what ails the world. In spite of your most noble efforts, old fellow, everyone involved with this story of good intentions has been punished—Lucy, her late husband, and the Grant Munros."

I joined Holmes in sampling the brandy. It gave me time to reflect on his words. Whether purposely or not, he had omitted my name from the list of victims. Obviously, it had not been I who had fired the newlyweds' home, and yet my role in the matter had led inexorably to the tragic conclusion.

As I have already indicated, for Sherlock Holmes the name of Norbury had come to signify a mistake. Ironically, it now seemed to serve the same purpose for me. However calculating Holmes's analysis of the affair might have sounded, I have to confess that he was correct about the logic of the situation. Had I not naively attempted to right society's wrongs, a young man would still be living, a mother and daughter would still be part of a happy household, and I myself would not be shrouded in gloom.

"But wait a moment," I told myself. "Had not Holmes picked himself up after Norbury all those years ago? Had he not just a few months later successfully solved the riddle of 'The Sign of Four', the adventure in which I met my own true love? Perhaps it was my longing for Mary Morstan that awakened in me the desire to see Lucy and Jos as happy as Mary and I had been.

To be sure, colour had played no role in *our* relationship. For a love like Jos and Lucy's to be so unencumbered, the planet would no doubt have to be populated by masses of grey figures instead of individual blacks and whites. Only then would colour, which now so conveniently functions to separate us all, no longer play a role in human relationships.

"To a world free from prejudice!" I suddenly cried out, raising my glass as I did so. However distant from our present-day existence, at the very least Lucy and Jos had taken a step towards such a future.

Holmes raised his glass as well. I believe I detected a glimmer of appreciation in his steel-grey eyes.

A Case of Mistaken Identity

No amount of fire or freshness can challenge
what a man will store up in his ghostly heart.
--F. Scott Fitzgerald
The Great Gatsby

I

*W*ith a furled black brolly hooked over my arm, I
stood outside my door in Queen Anne Street peering up and
down the road. It was the beginning of a cool, wet June in
the year 1924; and like many another evening that summer,
the air felt thick and heavy beneath grey and threatening
skies. To be sure, my sitting room offered more comfort;
but I was awaiting the arrival of a taxi and wanted to be as
punctual as possible.

Fortunately, I did not have long to wait. In a matter
of minutes a dark-blue cab rolled to a stop. A wave from
the rear-seat window assured me that my old friend was
inside; and employing the umbrella as a walking-stick, I
carefully made my way along the slippery flags to the kerb.

"Ah, my dear Watson," said Sherlock Holmes as I
planted myself upon the shiny black-leather cushion beside
him, "so good to see you."

Except for the silvering of his combed-back hair and
thick brows, Sherlock Holmes looked as he always had—the

same square jaw, the same aquiline nose, the same steely glance from those sharp, grey eyes.

"Holmes," said I, "you haven't aged a bit."

"As much as one may hope for the contrary, old fellow," said he indicating his grey hair, "one cannot cheat the calendar—let alone the occasional touch of rheumatism."

It was always a pleasure to see my former colleague and companion. And yet, though Holmes and I had not visited with each other for quite some time, I confess to having felt mystified at his quick acceptance of my dinner-invitation. Only the day before had I asked him to dine with another guest and me at the Langham, and I really did not expect him to come up to London from his cottage upon the South Downs on such short notice. Yet here he was.

Holmes must have realised what I was thinking. Perhaps he even sensed my resentment at his failure to keep me abreast of his recent adventures. For no sooner had the taxi lurched forward than he drew a small white envelope from an inner-coat pocket and slid it tantalisingly across the seat in my direction. Though the ride to nearby Portland Place would be brief, he had obviously concluded that there would be sufficient time for me to discern the significance of the envelope's contents and presumably the reason for his last-minute trip to London.

First things first, however. I noted his Sussex address scrawled across the front of the envelope and three American stamps affixed to the upper-right-hand corner bearing a postmark from New Brunswick, New Jersey. Yet what most intrigued me was the crimping at the centre of the envelope formed by the small objects within. Somehow, it all seemed distantly familiar.

Sherlock Holmes nodded at the thing. "Open it," said he.

"Open it?" I repeated, making certain that I had heard him correctly.

He nodded, and so I picked up the envelope. It took but a moment of fingering the tiny pieces within to guess the contents. Indeed, once I had lifted the flap, I was not at all surprised to discover the five small pips. Although from previous experience, I expected to see the whitish, dried seeds from an orange, these pips were brown, and I judged them to have come from an apple. Printed in red ink on the inside of the envelope's flap were the words, "Drop the case"; beneath them, the letters K.K.K.

"A copycat?" I chuckled, employing the American term. I vaguely remembered a similar message we had received in the late 80's some four decades ago. It was my initial introduction to the Ku Klux Klan, the secret American society primarily bent on terrorising Negroes—and worse. Readers may remember my account of the affair, which I titled "The Five Orange Pips".

For his part, Holmes appeared unamused, reacting to my light-hearted response with a tightening of his jaw and a narrowing of his eyes. "I received this envelope by post a few days ago," said he. "How they got my address I have no idea, but it is the reason that I agreed so quickly to join you and your friend for dinner this evening."

"He's not exactly my friend, Holmes," I protested as the taxi rolled to a stop before the many-faceted Langham. "He's a writer—an American actually. As I explained in my wire, I met him just yesterday. That's when he told me he hoped to speak with you as soon as possible about a murder in New Jersey—"

A doorman in grey livery cut me off in mid-sentence.

"Welcome to the Langham," said he, opening the door of the taxi and gesturing to the front arch of the building's three-sided stone portico.

Before I could get up, Holmes grabbed my arm and pulled me towards him. "*Two* murders, actually," he whispered close to my ear and snatched the envelope from my hand.

Two murders—Holmes was right. He may not have known the man we were about to meet, but he certainly knew about the case the man had told me about. Yet owing to both the doorman and my stick-like umbrella, I managed to exit the cab without saying a word. Holmes paid the driver, and together the two of us walked slowly through the familiar entrance hall and into the vestibule that led to the *Salle á Manger*.

Our short trek did nothing to stifle my curiosity. We passed various small tables where patrons were taking coffee, their hushed voices accompanied by some nondescript melodies offered by classical players stationed in a corner of the broad hallway. Holmes seemed to enjoy the tunes, but I would not be distracted. In spite of the music, my thoughts were haunted not only by the meaning of those pips Holmes had showed me but also by whatever connection they might have to the murders to which he had referred. For that matter, I now worried that we ourselves might be in some danger.

"Mozart's G major String Quartet," observed Holmes with a brief but self-satisfied smile. "Though the second violin is a bit off."

Under the circumstances, I admired his calm. Here he was thinking about a fiddle whilst I was worrying about our safety. At the same moment Holmes was turning his head towards the musicians, I was considering a look over my shoulder for secret assassins.

Upon entering the dining room, a large darkened hall bordered by stately marble columns on facing walls, I offered our names to the *maître d'*; and he quickly ushered us to a well-appointed table set for three. It was there that the American I had mentioned to Holmes sat awaiting our arrival. In the tall glass he was clutching, a green half-rind of lime lay submerged in a pool of melted ice—no doubt the remains of a gin rickey, a drink that he had previously described to me. When he cast his eyes upon Holmes, a look of relief seemed to bathe the American's face.

Apparently, it was left to me to appreciate the irony. Though the entire business had begun in my own house the day before, Sherlock Holmes seemed much more aware of what was going on than did I. Apple pips? The Klan? Murders in New Jersey? Of all this, I remained as ignorant as I was the previous morning when I had been working innocently at my desk and the bell at the front door clanged for attention at precisely ten o'clock.

*****

"An American gentleman to see you, Dr Watson," said my young housekeeper, Miss Ross.

I smiled at her from behind a stack of papers. The older I grow, the more I appreciate how casting one's eye on an attractive young woman each day serves as a better tonic than any diurnal medicine I can name.

"Quite a good-looking fellow, sir," she added, "if you don't mind my saying. He said to tell you he's a writer."

"A writer?" I repeated, cupping my hand behind my ear to amplify the sound. I was always surprised when my accounts of Holmes's cases attracted the literary world. But I suppose it was why—now in my early seventies—I was still hard at work compiling portfolios of those sketches of mine that had most recently been published in The Strand. *My agent, Sir Arthur Conan Doyle, had already bestowed a title upon the volume I was currently completing: "The Case-Book of Sherlock Holmes". If authors like this fellow at the door were coming to see me from as far away as the United States, there seemed little doubt that my new collection would generate strong interest.*

In all honesty, however, I should inform my readers that I really do expect "The Case-Book" to be the last. My hearing problem is but one of the physical ailments with which I must contend. Alas, I no longer move as dextrously as I once did and, as a result, spend most of my days on the ground floor of my house. Due to this lack of mobility, my sitting room looks more like a library, my grand mahogany desk at its centre, surrounded by walls of bookshelves reaching to the ceiling.

When I go out walking, I employ a stick; and Miss Ross aids me in climbing the stairs. In fact, I confess rather sheepishly that it is her physical support pressing against my body that encourages me to ascend the staircase more often than might seem necessary. In any event, since the death of my wife, I have appreciated having Miss Ross about the place. She leaves me dinner before going home.

"Sir?" said she, her voice a degree louder as she awaited my instructions regarding the visitor at the door.

"Show the man in," said I, rising from my chair.

In spite of my other infirmities, my eyesight remains sharp; and I could see that Miss Ross was quite correct about the visitor's good looks. Advancing towards me was a dapper young man probably not yet thirty. At first, I took him to be clean-shaven; but the nearer he came, the more apparent was the hint of a feeble blond moustache. I placed him at about five-foot-eight, his short legs limiting his height. The tan he bore indicated that he had not been spending his summer in London; yet his stylish suit of white linen set off by a light-blue tie suggested he seemed undeterred by our continually-dreary English skies.

Though the gentleman caller had fairly bounded into the room, I immediately sensed the contradictions. He may have greeted me with a friendly smile; but his sad, green eyes betokened vulnerability. His brushed-back blond hair, sharply chiselled nose, and thin lips presented quite a handsome portrait; yet one could detect an aura of insecurity.

Holding a straw boater in his left hand, he extended his right in my direction. "Scott Fitzgerald," said he in his flat American accent. "My friends call me Fitz."

"John Watson," said I, shaking his hand, "but then you know who I am since you've come here to see me."

"Spot on," said my guest.

Whilst Miss Ross took the man's hat, I gazed at my striking visitor. I knew the name, of course: F. Scott Fitzgerald—the author of countless short stories; inventor of the phrase, "The Jazz Age"; composer of two successful novels, This Side of Paradise *and* The Beautiful and Damned. *More to the point, even I, cooped up as I was here in Queen Anne Street, had heard some of the more egregious tales from New York about the man and his wife—riding atop the bonnets of taxis, bathing in pubic fountains, disrobing at parties—and always, in spite of the prohibition against alcohol in the States, the constant drinking. To be* sure, much of his work had received positive reviews, yet I personally had no intention of exposing myself to his sordid descriptions of colonial sensationalism.

In spite of my protests, however, let it not be thought that I am in the habit of shunning American writers. Faithful readers will recall that I have fraternised with such figures in the past—people like Clemens and Crane and London. Yet those encounters had taken place many years before, and all had something to do with crimes for my detective-friend to solve. With Holmes now comfortably retired, I had no idea—other than the desire to meet the biographer of Sherlock Holmes, of course—what might have pushed so infamous a figure as F. Scott Fitzgerald in my direction.

"Might I offer you some refreshments?" said I, waving in the general direction of the silver tea and coffee pots.

"Normally, I don't drink in the morning," said Fitzgerald with what sounded like a bit too much piety. "But," he added with what I regarded as equally too much enthusiasm, "I wouldn't say no to a gin rickey."

My blank expression elicited an explanation.

"An American drink, Doctor—gin, carbonated water, and half a lime."

My housekeeper moved to serve him, but I intervened. "It's all right, Miss Ross. We'll manage on our own."

"Very good, sir," said she, casting one final look at the handsome visitor as she gently closed the door on her way out.

To fulfil Fitzgerald's early-morning craving for spirits, I pointed him in the direction of the cherry-wood sideboard. Upon it stood my silver tantalus and its three bottles, one of which contained a smooth gin. For the carbonated water, he would have to rely on my ancient gasogene.

"There's ice in the bucket," I told him, "but I'm rather afraid you'll need to substitute lime juice for an actual lime. Could you pour me a glass of water while you're at it?"

I moved to the wing chair opposite the sofa whilst Fitzgerald filled our glasses. Placing the drinks on the table between us, he seated himself across from me and sampled his rickey with a satisfied smile.

"Now, Mr Fitzgerald, what brings you to London?" I asked, fully expecting some sort of homage to my literary accomplishments.

"It's simple really," said he. "I need to meet with Sherlock Holmes."

"Holmes!" I cried, my eyebrows shooting up in astonishment. Although I had been compiling a number of our adventures together, it had been quite a while since I had given serious thought to actually engaging with my old friend again.

Fitzgerald ran a hand through his luxuriant hair. "You see, Doctor, I'm in the middle of writing my third novel. Actually, I've been working on it for some time. I call it Among Ash Heaps and Millionaires."

I reacted not at all to the cumbersome title, and Fitzgerald immediately recognised my response as unspoken criticism.

"You know," said he with a quick laugh, "I'm not too keen on the title either. That's why I have alternatives. In fact, as of this moment, thanks to you I'm going to start calling it Trimalchio in West Egg."

I continued staring blankly. "Trimalchio? West Egg?" The terms meant nothing to me.

189

"West Egg is my fictional name for Great Neck. It's a town on Long Island in New York. We rented a house there, and I studied the inhabitants. As for Trimalchio, he was a Roman slave who got rich through underhanded means. At least, that's what Petronius says in the Satyricon. *"*

Fitzgerald completed this announcement with a broad grin. Though he was obviously proud to show off his knowledge of the Classics, I greeted this explanation with no more emotion than I had displayed just moments before.

"It doesn't really matter," Fitzgerald said, dismissing my ignorance with a measured wave of his glass and a quick shake of his head. The point is that the fellow's a model for the main character in my novel. It's about a rich American crook and the married woman he falls in love with." He paused to sample his rickey. "But to be honest," he said with a lick of his lips, "even though I completed a first draft, my life in New York—it's not called the den of iniquity for nothing, you know—the city had gotten the best of me. I figured that if I was ever to complete the book, I'd have to go some place where there was peace and quiet."

This observation made sense to me, and I nodded accordingly.

"We have to watch our money," Fitzgerald continued, " but thanks to what I'd earned from my magazine stories, Zelda and I—Zelda's my wife—packed up our belongings—including our little girl Scottie (she's two)—and we sailed to France in early May. It took us ten *days to get from New York to Paris!* Ten *days on a 'dry steamer', the* Minnewaska. Ten days without a drink! *Can you imagine? In fairness, I guess I've been making up for it ever since." Here he held up his glass to illustrate the*

point—as if I needed such a gesture to recognise an inebriant.

"But Paris?" I said in disbelief. "Why, the cost alone—"

"Oh," he smiled, "we didn't remain there—not in Paris. You don't stay in Paris if you're trying to economise. For that matter, you don't come to London either—believe me. But we bought an inexpensive car and drove south to the Riviera. It sounds swell, but it's pretty empty in the summer. Apparently, the French consider the Riviera a place to spend the winter. As a result, we were able to rent a small house a few miles north of St. Raphaël."

"Quite beautiful, I should imagine."

Fitzgerald fairly beamed. "Our house—it's called Villa Marie—*stands on a pine-shaded hill overlooking the town of Valescure and the glorious too-blue Mediterranean. It's hot in the daytime under that flaming sun; but at night, when the liquid dark comes down, it's perfect. Mainly though, it's cheap—$79 a month—and silent—if you discount the rush of the sea. It's a place where I can work on the book and not be disturbed. Zelda spends her time on the sand with a couple of French aviators she's met."*

I drank some water while picturing the paradisiacal scene. But too much time had already elapsed without my having asked the inevitable question: "What in the world does any of this have to do with Sherlock Holmes?"

Again Fitzgerald brushed at his hair. "I need some technical help with the plot of my novel, you see. As of now, it contains at least two murders and a suicide."

"'Two murders and a suicide,' I repeated to be sure I had heard him correctly. "And how, may I ask, could a fictional work of such a nature possibly involve Sherlock Holmes?"

Fitzgerald held up his glass to me, as if to say,
"Good question." Then he drank some more. "I was
hoping Holmes might advise me. You see, I've re-worked
much of the story. Ever since the failure of a play I wrote,
I've been worrying more about Trimalchio—*the book, I*
mean. My original plan was to deal with the impact of the
Catholic Church on the life of a little boy. I was raised
Catholic. That's probably why the early effects of sin and
guilt intrigue me."

F. Scott Fitzgerald thinks too much, *I mused.*

"But lately I've been looking for a new angle.
Forget about the little boy. I want to say more about the
evil schemes those sins produce in adults—you know, crimes
and such. It's funny. I've always liked Chesterton's Father
Brown mysteries. Maybe that's why. You know, back in my
youth, I wrote a murder-mystery myself. I guess I've been
fascinated by curious deaths from the start, and that's what
led me to writing about real-life murders."

"'Real-life murders'? I thought your book was
fiction."

"It is," Fitzgerald nodded. "But as it so happened,
Zelda and I moved from St. Paul to New York in '22—just
when news of two horrific killings in New Jersey were
appearing in the local newspapers.

"Mind you, I'm not in the business of writing crime
stories; but to establish my Trimalchio *as a product of that*
era, I decided to include references to actual events—the
fixing of our baseball World Series, for instance; and I offer
indirect allusions to Presidential hijinks as well as scenes of
people skirting our anti-drinking laws." Here, with a
decided twinkle in his eyes, he held up his glass again.

"And?"

"And for the accuracy of the historical record, I want part of the plot to be propelled by that real-life—and as yet unsolved—pair of hard-boiled murders in New Jersey. I've kept some newspaper clippings about them in my scrapbook."*

"I'm beginning to understand what you're after," said I—*though what Holmes might have to do with a two-year-old double-murder in America, I could only guess. Affairs of a literary nature were not the sort of issue with which to bother my friend.*

"You see, Doctor, I've reached a kind of impasse. I'm dissatisfied with Trimalchio's sixth and seventh chapters, the ones that establish the motives for the murders. I'm worried that some of it is too raw. That's why I want Sherlock Holmes to tell me more about the realities of the case—mainly, what he knows about the people involved. I want to avoid having to fall back upon the usual trashy imaginings I've based much of my other work on."

"Look here, Mr Fitzgerald—" said I.

"Fitz," he reminded me with a winsome smile. *Then quickly downing the rest of his rickey, he raised the empty glass.*

"May I?" he asked.

I nodded once more in the direction of the tantalus, then resumed my argument: *"Sherlock Holmes is retired. He is no longer fighting crime. And though he may have read something of this case you have in mind—"*

---

* Fitzgerald's interest in the aforementioned murders is substantiated by Sarah Churchwell in her 2013 study titled *Careless People: Murder, Mayhem, and the Invention of The Great Gatsby*. It must be pointed out, however, that she makes no mention of Sherlock Holmes's role in the investigation. (DDV)

"The Hall-Mills murders," Fitzgerald said over his shoulder while pouring more gin.

I cupped my hand behind an ear and asked him to repeat the names.

"They mean nothing to me," I murmured after he had done so. "And I would be very surprised indeed if they mean anything more to Sherlock Holmes—other than what he may have read about them in the newspapers. Besides, he and I have been out of touch."

Fitzgerald's response surprised me. "I'll say you've been out of touch! I realise that it hasn't been reported, Doctor, but still . . . you don't seem to know that Sherlock Holmes himself went to New Jersey back in December of '22 to investigate the very same murders we're talking about."

Holmes in America? Two years before and not a word to me? *(At least, I could not remember that he had informed me of such a trip.)*

"How is it, Mr Fitzgerald," I asked with not a little envy, "that you have come to know of Holmes's involvement?"

The American took another pull of his gin. "Actually, I inferred as much from the comments of Sir Basil Thomson in the New York Times.*"*

I had met Sir Basil on some occasion or another. A former head of the CID at Scotland Yard, he kept a sharp eye out for Holmes—both to learn from and to criticise. He was the type of rigorous investigator that many an objective observer of the Yard has called the embodiment of Holmes himself.

"You see," Fitzgerald explained, "like Holmes, Thomson was also asked to evaluate the police proceedings in New Brunswick. He was in New York not long after

Holmes's investigation. You can look it up. Sir Basil never offered any specific solutions to the murders, but he had plenty to say about Sherlock Holmes. He rambled on and on about how the best police work involves a team—not soloists. It is organizations that solve actual mysteries, he maintained, not solitary detectives like Sherlock Holmes. Why, he even joked that if he himself had to rely on the same methods as those employed by Holmes, then he, Sir Basil Thomson, might very well lock up the Archbishop of Canterbury by mistake." *

I had to smile. It was exactly the sort of comment one would expect from a Yarder.

"I tell you, Doctor, you could just smell the rivalry. The more Thomson devalued Holmes, the more convinced I became that Holmes must actually have investigated the affair. You just knew *it! Once I incorporated the murders into my novel, I figured a private eye like Sherlock Holmes would be just the fellow to fill me in on the details. After my contacts at the* Times *confirmed that Holmes had been to New Jersey to study the case, I knew I had to talk with him."*

I drank more water.

"Max Perkins, my editor at Scribner's, contacted Conan Doyle to find out where you live. I left Zelda and Scottie at Villa Marie *so I could pop over to London for a couple of days to see you. What better way to get a hold of Sherlock Holmes than by having his noted Boswell make the connection?"*

---

* Thomson's comments regarding the Archbishop of Canterbury and Sherlock Holmes were made in a speech to the Royal Society of Arts and quoted in the *New York Times* of April 24, 1921. (DDV)

I blushed at the compliment. Still, I had to repeat that, thanks to my questionable health, Holmes and I had not communicated since his trip to New Jersey.

"Look, Doctor," Fitzgerald said, motioning with his glass to emphasise his point, "all I ask is that you give him a call."

"He has no telephone."

"Send him a wire then, saying I'd like to see him, and arrange a visit. I'm staying at the Langham. We could meet there for dinner."

"The Langham?"

"I know, I know. I said we were trying to avoid spending too much, but you can't deny that there's always a high cost to economising. Tell Mr Holmes that to get his personal view of the case, I'd travel anywhere that would be convenient for him. I mean—it's obvious that he still gets around. Recall that it wasn't so long ago that he was in the States."

F. Scott Fitzgerald offered a persuasive argument. Obviously, Holmes did indeed "get around"—with or without my knowledge. I must admit that his failure to notify me *of his trip continued to sting. After all, was I not—as Fitzgerald had pointed out—Holmes's faithful Boswell? As such, should I not have been given an opportunity to record Holmes's investigation into these infamous murders?*

Why *not* take advantage of Fitzgerald's interest in the crimes? *Fitzgerald had said the murders were unsolved, and yet Holmes was not the sort to leave such matters up in the air. Why not use Fitzgerald's request as an excuse to hear about the murders from Holmes himself? Perhaps I might even discover an opportunity to add one final sketch to "The Case-Book".*

Truth be told, as a writer, I also felt sympathetic towards Fitzgerald's literary plight. I cannot ignore my good fortune at having actually been to most all of the locations I have recreated in my accounts, locations like Baskerville Hall, Stoke Moran, the Copper Beeches. At the very least, it seemed to me that Fitzgerald deserved to hear the perspective of one who had studied these murders first-hand. And yet at the same time, I still found it difficult to imagine Sherlock Holmes conversing with so flamboyant a figure as F. Scott Fitzgerald about so trivial a matter as a book of fiction.

My guest mustered a winsome, almost seductive, grin. "Give it a try, Doctor. That's all I ask. Contact Sherlock Holmes. Let me pick his brain."

In the end, the young man was quite persuasive—not to mention my own desire to see Holmes again. Besides, at the very least, I would be familiarising myself with a two-year-old mystery that—as far as I knew at the time—seemed to still want untangling. I knew nothing about this Hall-Mills murder case, but the act of examining any unsolved crime has always fired my imagination.

"All right," I told Fitzgerald. "I'll give it a go."

With an appreciative smile he held up his now-empty glass in a form of salutation.

*****

Upon seeing Holmes and me approach, the American rose to greet us.

"Mr Fitzgerald," said I by way of introduction, "may I present to you Mr Sherlock Holmes."

The American surprised me by bending at the waist in an almost formal bow. Only after he straightened up, did the young man speak. "Thanks for meeting me on such quick notice, Mr Holmes."

With a wave of his hand, my friend brushed away the appreciative words. "I've worked with writers before, Mr Fitzgerald," he offered as we settled into our seats, "though never, I confess, in so appropriate a setting."

"How so?"

"Why, this is the very room in which Oscar Wilde and Watson's agent, Conan Doyle, had their famous dinner in August of '89."

"1889?" Fitzgerald marvelled. "Why, I wasn't even born yet."

"Who was the host, Watson? Another American if I remember rightly."

"To be sure. They met with Joseph Stoddart, the managing editor of an American periodical—*Lippincott's,* I believe. Conan Doyle called the affair a 'golden evening'."

"As well he might," observed Holmes to Fitzgerald. "Prompted by that dinner party, Wilde composed *The Picture of Dorian Gray*, and Conan Doyle was able to coax a lengthy narrative out of friend Watson here. Which case was it, old fellow?"

"*The Sign of Four.*"

"Quite so," said Holmes. "Who can forget the perilous chase up the Thames on the trail of Jonathan Small and the Andaman Islander with the poisonous darts?"

Who can forget indeed? I thought. But my mind focused on different memories of the case, for it was during that same investigation all those years ago that I met Miss Mary Morstan, the beautiful young woman who was destined to become my bride. Following her death, I thought I could never marry again. Fortunately, I was wrong.

Fitzgerald broke into my reverie. "As Dr Watson may have informed you, Mr Holmes, it's of a more recent case I wish to speak—the Hall-Mills murders." Suddenly, Fitzgerald snapped his fingers, and a waiter immediately approached our table. "But first we must fortify ourselves."

Holmes and I leaned back in our chairs.

"Drinks, gentlemen," commanded the writer. "It's all on me—or on my publisher. 'Get the damned book finished!' I've been told in no uncertain terms. Perkins assures me that Scribner's regards any money they advance me to that end as a good investment."

Holmes and I each ordered a sherry; Fitzgerald, another gin rickey.

"I've got to tell you, Mr Holmes," said the American after the drinks were delivered, "that I was most pleased you agreed to meet with me. You have quite the reputation for shunning interviews."

Holmes raised his long forefinger. "Don't press your luck, Mr Fitzgerald. Let it not be thought that I am here to promote your career. I have reason enough to keep these murders in the public eye."

Recalling the apple pips Holmes had just shown me, I understood his desire to get to the bottom of the matter.

"I regard neither murder nor its investigation as a subject of frivolity," Holmes explained. "Watson here can tell you how often I used to remonstrate with him for pandering to public tastes. He constantly romanticised our enquiries when he should have been presenting them as austere models for criminal study. But in New Jersey, Mr Fitzgerald, my confidential findings were dismissed so quietly that I'm hoping your novel might gain them further exposure.

"Call me 'Fitz'," said the writer, hoisting his glass with a wink of an eye.

Sherlock Holmes ignored the invitation.

"What I am truly hoping, Mr Fitzgerald," said he, "is that your book will trigger a new investigation and reveal not only what happened to the minister and the choir singer, but also some other activities of a criminal nature possibly committed by the killers."

I shook my head. "I'm afraid I'm in the dark. What minister? What choir singer? For that matter, Holmes, I had no idea that you had actually gone to America over this affair until Fitzgerald informed me of the fact. You might at least have told me of your plans. I'm a bit hurt."

"You're quite right, of course, old fellow," said Holmes. "I'm sorry about that." He sampled his sherry— no doubt to avoid the discomfort of offering further apology. "Neither one of us is getting any younger, old fellow, and Conan Doyle has told me how occupied you've been compiling your stories. Why, I had no idea if my own antiquated skills would even be helpful in the New Jersey investigations."

Fitzgerald held his glass up to Holmes as if to toast him. "You underestimate yourself, Mr Holmes."

"So what happened?" I asked, my injured pride quickly replaced by curiosity.

"I too am most interested in hearing your view of things," said Fitzgerald, "but hedonist that I am, I insist that we order our meals before you begin."

Once again, the American summoned the waiter with a snap of his fingers. I looked at Holmes who simply rolled his eyes at Fitzgerald's brashness. Still, the *table d'hôte* menu sounded appealing, and I ordered the rack of lamb; Holmes, the *coq au vin*; and Fitzgerald, the roast beef.

No sooner did the waiter depart than Fitzgerald produced from inside a jacket pocket a small notebook and gold pencil. "At the risk of stating the obvious, gentlemen," said he, "I find it vitally important to take notes about all sorts of things—especially when those things have a direct relationship to my current work."

For his part, Sherlock Holmes took a moment to study the remaining sherry in his glass, sipped a bit, and then began his narrative.

II

"From the start," said Holmes, "I followed the Hall-Mills case in the daily newspapers. It was not without its curiosities. Conan Doyle himself was mentioned by Charlotte Mills, the sixteen-year-old daughter of the murdered woman—"

"The one the papers call a 'flapper'," interrupted Fitzgerald. "She caught my interest."

"Quite so," said Holmes curtly. Never pleased at being cut off in mid-sentence, he began again. "It seems the girl had been reading *The New Revelation*, Sir Arthur's book on spiritualism, and hoped to converse with her deceased mother. The daughter wanted to ask her just who was responsible for the crimes. Needless to say, such a strategy never materialised—if you can forgive the pun."

Fitzgerald offered a polite smile.

"But to the case itself: In early December of 1922, I was invited by Mr Wilbur Mott, the New Jersey state prosecutor, to come to America. He sought my opinion of a mystery that had occurred some two months before. It seems that a pair of grisly murders had been committed just outside of New Brunswick, a quiet town situated on the banks of the Raritan River. As one can imagine, in so idyllic a setting the occurrence of such a heinous crime was rare—but then, sad to say, so were the authorities' preparations for investigating it.

"Confusion reigned from the start. In fact, it took the state about a month to discover that jurisdictional issues were severely hampering the investigation. Deciding whose case it was posed the first challenge. The bodies were found in a field in Somerset County, you see; and yet it was widely believed that the victims had been killed somewhere in the town of New Brunswick, which is in the county of Middlesex. To resolve the problem, New Jersey's Attorney General appointed a state prosecutor to oversee the enquiry."

"This fellow Mott," I observed, "the chap who contacted *you*, Holmes."

"Just so. In fact, most of what I am about to tell you I learned from him and from the ocean of papers comprising the police report that he provided.

"Do tell, Mr Holmes," said Fitzgerald, pencil poised. "We're all ears."

"The murders in question occurred on a quiet Thursday night, the 14th of September. Although the police detected bits and pieces of evidence, they found nothing conclusive. Oh, a few peripheral suspects were considered, but on 5 December a Grand Jury announced that no indictments were to be brought against anyone. It was this frustrating result that prompted Mr Mott to seek fresh eyes."

"And so he turned to *you*," I prompted.

"Precisely—although I should add that he made it quite clear from the start that anything I might discover could never be attributed to Sherlock Holmes. 'Public funds,' Mr Mott said, 'require our public servants to do the work themselves.'"

"You'd get no credit?" Fitzgerald asked.

Holmes chuckled drily. "'Getting the credit', as you call it, Mr Fitzgerald, has never been my need. As friend Watson has documented elsewhere, I prefer to work anonymously. Even in retirement, it is the problem itself that attracts me—the more complicated, the more attractive. I've dabbled in some interesting cases since leaving Baker Street—my work during the Great War and that business with the so-called 'Lion's Mane' come to mind—but not for a long time have I involved myself in so intricate a murder investigation as the one presented to me in New Jersey.

"Suffice it to say, I readily accepted the opportunity to put my analytical skills back to work. In fact, it was with an enthusiasm that surprised even me that, after securing a neighbour to look after my bees, I employed the Cunard line to convey me across the Atlantic."

At this provocative instant, the waiter arrived with our dinners. I must report, however, that savoury though the bill of fare was, not even the fine cuisine of the Langham could distract us from Holmes's compelling narrative. My friend did pause to butter some bread—a dramatic bit of theatre, perhaps, since once he had fully lathered it, he set the slice down uneaten.

Holmes also allowed himself a moment to sample the chicken. But after a few bites and an approving nod, he resumed his tale. "I met Mr Mott as soon as I was established in my hotel in New Brunswick. A distinguished-looking jurist in his sixties with iron-grey hair, he seemed just the man to set matters straight. And indeed he wasted no time before filling me in on the general background of the case.

"'On Saturday, the 16th of September,' he told me, 'a young New Brunswick couple went out for a morning stroll. Their walk took them through the ankle-deep grass of a field just outside of town—part of an abandoned farm where lovers are wont to amble, especially at night—that is, they did before these murders took place.'"

"I've studied the area," Fitzgerald interjected. "It's just south of a park called 'Buccleuch'. I like the name. In fact, I'm using it as an ancestral patronymic for the narrator of my novel."

"Quite so," responded Holmes, clearly uninterested in the development of Fitzgerald's fiction.

"The couple's excursion," Holmes went on, "turned out to be far different from the idyllic walk the two had been expecting. It was these two, you see, who stumbled across a pair of bodies lying among a scattering of trees. In fact, the feet of the corpses were pointing towards a nearby crab-apple tree."

"I assume that's important," said I, thinking of the pips Holmes had had shown me earlier.

He held up his hand, palm outward. "In due time," said he with a quick smile.

"The dead were Reverend Edward Wheeler Hall, the rector of New Brunswick's Protestant Episcopal Church of St. John the Evangelist, and Mrs Emily Mills, a member of the church choir. Hall, husband of the wealthy Frances Noel Hall, was in his early forties; Mrs Mills, wife to James Mills, the janitor and sextant of Reverend Hall's church, in her mid-thirties. The state prosecutor admitted that the causes of death were so obvious—the reverend had been shot in the head and Mrs Mills in the face—that the authorities had accepted the morticians' reports without requiring any official examinations of the bodies. In point of fact, formal autopsies had been dispensed with. As a result, the precise extent of the wounds wasn't discovered for weeks."

"No autopsies?" the doctor in me exclaimed. "Unforgiveable."

"I said much the same, old fellow. One can only assume that upon their arrival at the murder scene, the investigators had been so overly distracted by the gruesome tableau set out before them that they forgot their usual protocol.

"You see, gentlemen, as Mr Mott described it, 'Laid out in the grass on their backs as the bodies were, Mrs Mills's head rested on one of the Reverend's outstretched arms; her hand lay on his upper leg, and his white Panama hat covered his face—with his glasses, we would soon discover, carefully mounted on his nose. Their clothing was neatly arranged on their persons, and their feet, as I have said, pointed towards the crab-apple tree. The police also found the Reverend's calling card—his name printed in Gothic lettering—placed upright against the bottom of one of his shoes; and love letters to the Reverend—written with pencil on cheap paper in the handwriting of Mrs Mills—had been scattered round the bodies.' I should add, gentlemen, that though both were married to others, it was common gossip that the two were romantically involved with each other."

"A vicar?" I gasped.

Fitzgerald smiled at my *naiveté*. "It is this illicit love affair that interests me," said he. "It's what I seek to explore in my novel—lovers who betray the people they are attached to."

Again Holmes failed to respond to the literary diversion.

"I trust the authorities came round to conducting regular autopsies," said I.

"Ah, Watson, ever the medical man. That is precisely what they did. A prosecutor from Middlesex was made responsible for the body of Mr Hall; a prosecutor from Somerset, for that of Mrs Mills. The same doctors performed both procedures."

"A pinch of consistency, at any rate," I observed

"Following the earlier problems, Mr Mott was pleased to report the new facts that emerged from the autopsies. 'We learned,' said he, 'that the .32 calibre bullet, which had entered Hall's head near his right temple, had exited at the back of his neck on the left side. Since the missile had clearly travelled downward, it can be inferred that the poor man had been shot from above."

"Perhaps he was praying," I suggested.

"Praying or otherwise," said Holmes, "he'd been on his knees and executed."

Interestingly, Fitzgerald seemed to pay little mind to the forensic details. He went right on eating as Holmes described the bloody details.

"Actually," said Holmes, "the remains of Mrs Mills proved more revealing. It turns out that she had been shot in the face not once—as had first been reported—but three times; and the scarf that had been wrapped round her neck had actually concealed the fact that her throat had been slashed from ear to ear. So deep was the cut that her head had been nearly severed."

"A veritable holocaust!" I cried. "And so many horrors missed! What sort of organisation do they run out there?"

"Quite so," Holmes murmured again.

"And who do the authorities think was responsible for this mayhem?" I asked. "They must have some ideas about the perpetrator of these atrocities."

"Yes," said Fitzgerald, pencil now at the ready, "those are the people I'm most interested in hearing your opinions of."

Holmes shook his head glumly. "Just the usual suspects, I'm afraid. As always, there were the wrong-headed possibilities—the young man who found the bodies; a vestryman who was in the area at the time. But the police reserved their hardest looks for the newly-widowed spouses."

"The initial suspects," I found myself pontificating, "whenever a husband or wife is killed."

"And yet," offered Fitzgerald as he sliced into another healthy portion of beef, "I've read that the husband, Jimmy Mills, is too dumb to have planned such a crime. In my *Trimalchio*, I say he's so dumb that he doesn't even know he's alive."

"Be careful," cautioned Holmes. "Stupidity is one of the most effective guises a guilty person can don—though I must agree that in the case of the cuckolded Mills, I believe you have read him correctly. From all the reports, such a characterization credibly excuses the man. No, from the start, the prime suspect has always been the affluent widow—Mrs Frances Noel Hall."

"The wife did it then!" I exclaimed, waving my fork, "just as I said."

Holmes placed his hand on my wrist to calm me down. "We have an alleged key witness," said he, "to thank for the identification—a Mrs Gibson, who claims to have been in the vicinity."

"The pig woman," offered Fitzgerald.

"You know of her then," said Holmes, releasing my arm.

"Oh, yes. They call her that because she raises pigs on her farm."

"Well," said Holmes, "on the night in question, she thought someone had been stealing the corn from that farm; and to have a look, she rode out to her field on a mule. She claimed that it was then that she had heard four shots and, thanks to the moonlight, seen a white-haired woman in a tan coat—a description of Mrs Hall—and three other men. She went so far as to say that someone had called out 'Henry', which happens to be the name of Mrs Hall's brother. He, along with a cousin and another brother—an eccentric the townspeople call 'Crazy Willie'—were also suspected."

Fitzgerald shook his head. "But lots of people doubted the 'pig woman's' account."

"That's correct," said Holmes. "There were too many discrepancies in her repetitions of the story. Mr Mott counted five people in one of her scenarios, six in another. She also said that the vicar had fallen when he'd been shot—yet thanks to the autopsy, as I've already pointed out, we know he was kneeling when he was killed. In short, some in authority believed her; others did not."

"What *is* the answer then?" I asked. "Whether this 'pig woman' was right or wrong, *somebody* killed those people. Who was responsible for committing such evil deeds?"

I knew I was sounding naïve once again, and Fitzgerald was quick to remind me.

"Surely, Dr Watson, a writer with your insights can detect the whiff of jealousy and revenge that hovers over a pair of marriages gone sour. In *Trimalchio*, I attribute more than one death to those same perfidious motivations."

Left to ponder Fitzgerald's fiction, we finished our meals, and the plates were removed. Both my dinner companions declined after-dinner sweets, but I could not resist the chocolate *gateau*.

III

Following the arrival of the coffee and my cake, Holmes began again. "I found myself at odds with Mr Mott. He tended to believe the Pig Woman; I didn't. I simply couldn't accept that Mrs Hall or members of her prominent family were involved. There were simply too many distracting clues suggesting otherwise. For instance, the prosecutor's conclusion ignored the role of the crab-apple tree. Why was it so important for the killer—or killers—to point the bodies in the direction of the tree? I had to see the area for myself, and I told Mr Mott so."

"'No point,' said he. 'Not only has the weather been terrible—we've just had some December snow—but large numbers of people have tramped all over the place—hundreds of gawkers. Why, one weekend in October we had over three hundred cars! The police did their best to preserve the original scene, but souvenir hunters put their fingers all over Hall's calling card and the scattered love-letters. Why, some enthusiasts have even ripped off the bark from the crab-apple tree for macabre mementos.'"

I shook my head in disbelief. *How could the police allow such confusion?* We used to think the Yarders made mistakes! Why, not even Lestrade could have bungled a crime scene so badly.

"Regardless of the prosecutor's caveats," said Holmes, "I refused to be gainsaid.

"The next day broke cold and bleak; but early that morning a black police motor-car conveyed Mr Mott and me through New Brunswick along the Easton Avenue streetcar line—beyond the shops and offices, past a few stylish houses—to the fields and farmlands at the outskirts of the town. By the time we reached Buccleuch Park where the trolley rails ended, the traffic had become very sparse indeed. Just past the columns fronting the Parker Home for the Aged, we turned left into De Russey's Lane. There remained but a short drive to the dirt road next to which the bodies had been found.

"As a precaution, a half dozen uniformed policemen stood by to keep the fields of the abandoned farm free of any wandering pedestrians. The show of force turned out to be unnecessary, however, for only a scattering of winter-thinned trees, their naked branches reaching skyward like brittle bones, interrupted the barren landscape.

"It required a single glance to confirm the contamination of the spot where the bodies had been discovered. The recent snow had saturated the area, and indiscriminate crowds had indeed stamped down the grass and marched over underbrush. Yet once Mr Mott pointed out the celebrated crab-apple tree, I knew that—manhandled as it had already been—here stood an entity that bulked large in the solution to the case."

"In what way?" Fitzgerald asked.

"Mind," said Holmes, "what I am about to tell you both I also told Prosecutor Mott. To this day he has made nothing of my findings, but I continue to believe that before long the case will be re-opened, my view will prevail, and—once for all—justice will be served."

"And precisely what *is* your view, Mr Holmes?" Fitzgerald persisted.

Sherlock Holmes placed his elbows on the white tablecloth and steepled his fingers together. It was a way he had when he wanted to draw attention to a meaningful observation. "As I have said before, the art of detection is merely 'systematised common sense'. The feet of the deceased were pointing to the crab-apple tree. Clearly, that tree was the spot where one had to begin in order to unravel this tangle.

"Even though much of the brownish-red bark had been stripped away, a close examination with my glass revealed a small cross that had been carved chest-high into the narrow trunk. Given the relative freshness of the cut, one could surmise the mark had been made at the time of the murders."

"Do you think the killings were religious in nature then?" I asked. "After all, this Mr Hall was a vicar."

"Perhaps. But there was more. You know my methods, Watson. I employed my lens to examine the ground where the bodies had been placed. In spite of the damage to the area, it was easy to note the lack of blood. In fact, with the investigating chemist having discovered only .08 of a pint of blood in the grass, it was elementary to conclude that Mrs Mills's horrific neck-wound had been administered post-mortem.

"But it was at the spot where the feet of the dead had rested that I concentrated my greatest efforts. Remember that the vicar's calling card had been found leaning against his shoes. It was in that location that I discovered what no one else had seen: mixed in with the scrambled dirt and grass, I counted five apple pips."

Apple pips again . . . .

"So what?" questioned Fitzgerald. "What's so strange about apple seeds being found near an apple tree?"

"True enough, Mr Fitzgerald," Holmes smiled, "except that these were seeds from the *Malus pumila*, the *common* apple tree, not from the *Malus coronaria*, the specific crab-apple tree near where the bodies had lain."

"Do you mean to say that you can actually tell the difference?" the writer asked.

"Oh, yes, with the aid of a magnifying lens. The seeds of the common apple tree are small, brown, flattened ovoids. Those of the crab-apple tree are smaller, redder, and more shiny."

Fitzgerald shook his head in amazement. "But what makes this so important?"

Holmes's eyes flashed as they always did when he was about to reveal a significant conclusion. "I believe that the apple seeds were transported to the scene by the killer—or killers—for distribution. This discovery, along with the cross carved into the tree, was enough for me. I told Mr Mott that I was ready to return to my hotel.

"You see, there was a witness named Frank Csister whom I wanted to question. His original testimony involved none of the major suspects, so the police had ignored it. A chauffeur by trade, he happened to be out on the road near the scene of the murders that night. I had read the account that he had furnished the authorities, and I wanted to interrogate him myself. To me, his was exactly the sort of report I wanted to hear more of. The police file informed me that Csister worked in a garage. Apparently, when he was not driving passengers about, he was repairing motor-cars."

"Lots to do with automobiles in this case, eh, Holmes?" I observed. "Chauffeurs, motor-ways, garages."

"It's America we're talking about, Dr Watson," said Fitzgerald. "My Trimalchio drives a 'circus wagon'. If the story took place in England, I'm sure I would have been writing about trains."

"Indeed," Holmes muttered and continued his narrative. "Mr Mott said he had heard all he needed to from Csister and declined to go along. So once the police deposited me at my hotel in New Brunswick, I hired a taxi for the drive to Bound Brook, the borough some ten miles to the northwest where Frank Csister worked.

IV

"I found the fellow in a small garage," said Holmes. "A ginger-haired man with inquisitive eyes and a full, red beard. He was adjusting the steering of an old Dodge touring model. He wore grease-covered overalls and a soiled flat cap.

"'Again?' he said when I told him that I wanted to ask him about the Hall-Mills murders. 'I've already talked to the cops. They don't think much of what I have to say.'

"None the less, he agreed to spend a few minutes with me and recommended coffee at the *café* next door."

"Funny," Fitzgerald interrupted, "in *Trimalchio* I put a Greek joint next to a garage."

Holmes would not be distracted. "Csister and I seated ourselves at a small wooden table with our coffees between us. 'What did you see that night, Mr Csister,' I asked, 'the night of the murders?'

"He put two cubes of sugar into his coffee and stirred. 'Like I told the cops,' he said after administering to his drink, 'a friend of mine and me was driving to Red Bank. We was on our way to the volunteer fireman's ball, you know. It was getting dark out there, but around 8.30 or so we saw a small, dust-covered car—maybe a Ford or a Dodge—parked by the side of the road. It wasn't too far

213

from where them bodies was found. It didn't have no license plate, and only one tail-light was on.'

"'I'm sure you've seen many a car by the side of the road. What was so curious about this one?'

"'Ha!' he laughed, 'take your choice—the tire that came flying out of one of the windows just as we drove past or the three Negroes who poured out after it. They were yelling and throwing their arms around. Well, we didn't want no trouble so we speeded up and got out of there.'

"The thought of disguises immediately crossed my mind. 'Were these men truly Negroes,' I asked, 'or might they have been white men wearing black face-paint?'

"Csister shook his head. 'I tell you, Mr Holmes, me and my partner didn't hang around long enough to find out. We didn't want to get robbed or nothing—know what I mean?'

"'Anything else?'

"'Well, about two hundred feet down the road we saw another car. This one was shiny; but just like the one we saw before, the rear end was lit up by a single tail-light, and it didn't have no license. Once I heard about them murders out there, I told all this stuff to the cops here in Bound Brook. They promised they'd give my story to the dicks in Somerset County, but no one's ever come to talk to *me* about it. From what *I* hear, others seen them cars too, but the cops told me that them other folks said the cars was there way later—that I must have been wrong about the time."

"'Couldn't the cars have been out there for a few hours?' I asked Csister. 'That would explain why you and the others could see them at different times.'

"'Sure. That's why I thought my story was important.' He sipped some coffee before making his final pronouncement. 'Guess I was wrong.'

"Csister had no more to tell. I thanked him for his help, paid for the coffees, and returned with the taxi to my hotel."

Staring into our own coffees Fitzgerald and I both sat pondering the story.

It was the writer who broke the silence. "So what was it that you learned, Mr Holmes? The apple seeds, the cross in the tree, the cars by the road. What gives?"

I had a good idea of what Holmes was suggesting, so I was prepared when my friend said, "Perhaps Watson can enlighten you. The answer lies within an old case of ours, one which he has already chronicled."

"'The Five Orange Pips'," I announced for a second time that evening. "An adventure which you yourself labelled 'grotesque', Holmes."

"Yes, I did. But you must not forget that on another occasion I also said that 'there is but one step from the grotesque to the horrible'. And in this new case—two killings, a slit throat, gunshots to the face—oh, I think that step to the horrible had been taken."

I agreed. Staring some forty years into the past, I recalled more clearly the murder of John Openshaw. In spite of the warnings provided by the orange pips, those harbingers of death sent out by the Ku Klux Klan, his was a death that Holmes and I had failed to prevent. And yet, horrible as it was, his drowning near Waterloo Bridge did not seem as awful as the ghoulish deaths in New Jersey.

"The Klan?" echoed Fitzgerald after I had pronounced the peculiar words. "What in the world could a bunch of clowns running around in white sheets have to do with these murders in New Jersey? The Klan was a nineteenth-century invention—an outgrowth of our Civil War. Its basic purpose was to menace Negroes in the South."

"Quite so," Holmes agreed, "but I'm sure that as an American, you must be aware of the group's resurgence. In 1915, in your state of Georgia, a preacher named Joseph Simmons created a new version of the so-called "Invisible Empire". With inspiration from a film called *The Birth of a Nation*, the Klan, no longer content with persecuting freed slaves, began targeting any kind of behaviour they deemed immoral.

"And it continues today. When they find such sinners, they frequently administer corrective measures. What's more, they do not confine themselves to what used to be the Confederacy. One can find this newly resurrected version of the Klan active throughout your East Coast and—more to the point—New Jersey in particular."

"When Zelda and I return home," said Fitzgerald, "I suppose we should watch our backs." He flashed that ambiguous look again—half serious, half jocular—and one could not be certain if he was joking or sincerely considering the safety of his family.

"It is my contention," Holmes announced, "that the publicly known relationship between Mr Hall and Mrs Mills was exactly the kind of *outré* behaviour that would attract the Klan and which the Klan would desire to correct."*

In spite of his suspicions, Holmes made no reference to the pips he had shown me in the taxi. It seemed clear that

---

* Holmes's analysis closely predicts that of civil rights lawyer William Kunstler in his 1964 account of the Hall-Mills murders titled *The Minister and the Choir Singer*. (DDV)

he had no intention of sharing that particular detail with Fitzgerald.

"But, Holmes," said I, "in our earlier investigation, the Klan sent out warnings before they killed someone. Remember that it was the arrival of the five orange pips that brought poor Openshaw to our door in the first place. You never mentioned any such warnings regarding the murders in New Jersey."

Holmes managed a chuckle. "There has been no discussion of warnings, old fellow, because the local authorities found none. Recall that the police said nothing about *any* apple pips, and they failed to regard the cross on the tree as a clue. They also chose to ignore the letters sent to Florence North, the lawyer for Charlotte Mills, the dead woman's daughter."

"The flapper," Fitzgerald reminded us with another wink.

Holmes cocked an eyebrow, but continued his explanation. "One of the letters said that in order to discover the identity of the killer, the attorney should locate the Klan members in the church of the late Reverend Hall. And when Miss North herself suggested that vigilantes might be responsible for killing her client's mother, a letter-writer warned that if the lawyer did not stop accusing groups like the Klan, then they just might have to give Miss North 'a taste of the same medicine we gave to Mrs Mills. Beware,' they warned, 'or you will see the fiery cross some night and get your due reward.'"

"My word," I murmured. Not only did Holmes's argument sound convincing, but it also rendered more ominous the threat to his own person conveyed via the apple pips.

"Motive, means, and opportunity," said Holmes, ticking off each word on his fingers. "It seems quite compelling that outside forces were the instigators of the Hall-Mills murders. I'm sure you'll agree, Mr Fitzgerald, that thanks to the proliferation of motorcars to which you have already referred, the Klan can move quite easily across state boundaries. The dirty car observed by Csister might well have picked up large quantities of soot and grime as it travelled some great distance. It would have been no trouble at all for Klansmen to have committed these outrages and then retreated to safer grounds. In such an instance, their tracks would be most difficult to follow."

Fitzgerald ran a hand through his hair. "Blaming some amorphous outfit like the K.K.K. might be all fine and good for actually solving the case," said he, his brow now furrowed, "but I'm writing a novel about thwarted love. It was precisely the *romantic* dilemma of the victims that attracted me to these murders in the first place. And now *you* want to replace the love story with a mundane morality drama played out by some prudish thugs. Regardless of what you think may really have happened, Mr Holmes, in my *Trimalchio* I hold a cuckolded lover responsible for the murders—maybe two such lovers now that I think about it."

"It's funny, Mr Fitzgerald," mused Holmes, "the prosecution in the Hall-Mills case was bent on proving exactly what you are suggesting. They couldn't blame the hapless husband, so they turned their attention to the widowed Mrs Hall."

Holmes may have felt that he had struck too harsh a tone; for when he spoke again, I detected a note of sympathy in his voice.

"If you try viewing the story through the eyes of the officials," he said to Fitzgerald, "you might see the entire affair as a case of mistaken identities. The wrong suspects accused? The wrong witnesses believed . . . ?"

"Mistaken identities," Fitzgerald mused. Suddenly, eyes flashing directly at Holmes, he cried out, "Of *course!* It's exactly the sort of wrong-headed conclusion a dim-wit like the husband in my book would jump to. *Mistaken identities*—just the thing!"

Quickly, he rose to his feet, tossed his serviette on the table, and turned to leave. "I must return to *Villa Marie* and resume my work on *Trimalchio*. You've made the resolution very clear to me, Mr Holmes."

With that, the young American threw some money on the table and bolted from the restaurant. Later we learned that he had returned to his room, collected his valise, and departed for France that very night.

"And the pips sent to you by the Klan?" I asked Holmes.

With the shake of his head, he dismissed the question. "Whoever sent that message must believe a new investigation will soon be under way. No doubt they want to prevent my involvement in it. But as I have already given my thoughts to the state prosecutor and have nothing left to say on the matter, I trust that I can safely ignore such threats. I am done with my part of the enquiry, Watson. My conclusions were never taken seriously, and thus I have vowed to Mr Mott—before I ever received those apple pips—to remain silent if the case is re-opened."

I breathed more easily and now returned my attention to the chocolate cake before me. A few minutes later, Holmes and I extended our evening in the plush environs of the Langham with a round of port and cigars.

V

As it turned out, Sherlock Holmes had correctly predicted a second investigation into the Hall-Mills murders. The new novel by F. Scott Fitzgerald, however, was completed before the proceedings began and remained unaffected by the new legal developments. As most readers may know, Fitzgerald had changed the book's title yet again just before it was published on 10 April 1925. Formerly called *Trimalchio,* the novel ultimately appeared in public as *The Great Gatsby.*

A few days after its publication, a package arrived by post from Scribner's. Getting round even less dextrously than a few years before, I was relieved to have Miss Ross bring it to my desk in the sitting room.

Within the brown shipping paper, I discovered a gift from Fitzgerald—a first printing of *The Great Gatsby.* What is more, it was complete with the haunting dust-jacket crafted by Spanish artist Francis Cugat, a dark-blue cover featuring the disembodied face of a woman from whose sad, kohl-lined eyes—their irises containing neatly concealed reclining nudes—falls a tear. Actually, there were two copies of the book in the delivery—one intended for me, and the other to be sent to Sherlock Holmes.

A hand-written note (whose notorious grammar and spelling I have taken the liberty to correct) accompanied the books. It read:

> *Hotel Tiberio, Capri*
> *March 12, 1925*

Dear Dr Watson:

Along with this note, I asked Maxwell Perkins to send two copies of my latest novel to you once it was published. One is for you, and the other, if you would be good enough to pass it along, is for Mr Holmes. All in all, though I'm still not satisfied with the title, The Great Gatsby—I still think I should have named it Trimalchio— the book looks awfully good to me. In fact, I think that the chapters I reworked in light of the help you and Mr Holmes furnished are among the best things I've ever done. Oh, I may not have recreated the specific details of the actual murders, but I do believe that I was faithful to the spirit of the dead lovers. As for Cugat's cover, I find it a delight, and Zelda agrees.

I hear that there are those in England who say that we Americans can't write this sort of thing. Believing that you and Mr Holmes are not among them, I offer you my thanks.

Like the books themselves, it was signed, *F. Scott Fitzgerald.*

*****

It might be comforting to believe—as Sherlock Holmes had hoped—that the publication of *The Great Gatsby* caused enough interest in the Hall-Mills case to account for the new trial that took place in 1926. Yet the fictional murders that appear at the end of the novel are so unlike the originals that not even the most perceptive reader could argue a connection. The truth is that Fitzgerald had written a tragic tale based on mistaken identities rather than a tawdry crime-drama dealing with a gang of vigilantes. I suspect such had been his intention from the start.

Would that I could report otherwise, but the new enquiry was initiated by no clarion call for justice. On the contrary, it was the testimony from a marital annulment case that prompted another look at the pair of gruesome murders.

Catalyst for the legal action had been the complaints of an aggrieved husband, who maintained that his wife had lied to him. What connected the issue to the Hall-Mills case was the fact that the wife who was accused of lying had been a maid in the home of Mr Hall, and the lie she was accused of telling was her claim to her husband that she knew nothing of Mrs Hall's involvement in the murders.

The former maid was now admitting that four years earlier she had, in fact, heard incriminating statements from Mrs Hall during a telephone conversation. The newly offered hearsay was all the authorities needed to get them started once more.

Resurrecting the testimony of The Pig Woman, a fresh prosecutor charged Mrs Hall, along with her two brothers and a cousin, with the double murders at the crab-apple tree. On this occasion, however, an actual trial was convened. And yet, though it lasted sixteen days, the ending turned out to be no different from the earlier Grand Jury's failure to indict.

In point of fact, I learned of the *dénouement* from Holmes himself. Employing the news as motivation for a trip to London, he journeyed from the South Downs to share with me the information he had received from Wilbur Mott, the former prosecutor of the case.

"All the defendants were found not guilty," reported Holmes as we sampled the tea and biscuits provided by Miss Ross. "Ultimately," Holmes explained, "the maid retracted her condemnation of Mrs Hall."

"So there's an end to it," said I.

"Hardly," Holmes scoffed. "Mr Mott said that there are many who still believe the testimony of The Pig Woman. Even though her own mother denounced her three times in the courtroom as a "liar", people remain outraged that the suspects were acquitted. Some are urging the case be sent to the Governor for further prosecution."

I shook my head.

"Still," offered Holmes, "given my personal view of the actual perpetrators, I'm happy to say that the majority of the public seem resigned to the unsatisfying conclusion. As long as no new evidence had been disclosed, no one in the Hall family could be convicted of the murders—let alone hanged for them."

"Hanged! Surely it would never have come to that."

"No, indeed," said Holmes. "In spite of the Klan's threat to me and my own oath to be silent—I would have interrupted the legal proceedings with my personal findings in order to prevent punishment from falling on the wrong heads."

"And yet," I felt compelled to add, "the miscreants responsible for these two murders, the killers from the Ku Klux Klan, seem to have got away with the proverbial perfect crime."

"Alas, Watson, that seems to be the case. But perhaps we can take comfort in the conclusion of our previous brush with the K.K.K. You will remember that those men, having escaped the justice of an earthly court, had to face a Higher Judge much sooner than they had expected. Recall the shattered stern-post that had been seen floating in the waves, remnants of the *Lone Star* of Savannah, the ship upon which they attempted to make their escape. As the Latin proverb goes, *Res nolunt diu male administrari*."

My eyes widened in hope of encouraging the translation.

"'Things refuse to be mismanaged for long', he announced obligingly. "It is a concept cited by the

American philosopher Emerson in making the case that the world is run according to compensation. What appears to go unpunished will indeed be punished in the end."

Let the philosopher have the last word. To me, the whole idea sounded like a comforting fancy to tell oneself after playing a losing hand. Glancing out the window at the lingering twilight, I bit into a chocolate biscuit and put the entire criminal business to rest. Better to spend whatever time I had left enjoying sweets in the company of my friend and colleague, Mr Sherlock Holmes.